His Secret Boss

Elizabeth Coldwell

Published by Accent Press Ltd 2014

ISBN 9781783752409

ONE

'You have to admit, Claudia, it'll be wonderful publicity for you …'

Gina paused, and took a sip from her cappuccino, waiting for my reaction. In the chair beside her, Hugo Murray of Wild Card Productions regarded me intently. According to Gina, Hugo had been anxious to speak to me pretty much since the day I'd taken over running the company.

I glanced out of the window. Three floors below us on St Martin's Lane, the traffic was its usual Friday snarl-up, and the pavement tables outside the café across the road were occupied by shoppers enjoying the first pleasantly warm afternoon of spring. As I contemplated the familiar scene, I gave myself some thinking time. Why, I wondered again, had I agreed to this meeting? With everything I had on my plate since Dad died, I didn't have time to get involved with some reality show; even if Gina assured me it would be as good as free advertising for us. When I'd asked her to beef up our PR strategy, I'd expected advertorials in the Saturday travel supplements, maybe being asked to put myself up for a sympathetic profile on the business pages. Not this.

1

Turning the chair back to face them both, I said, 'So tell me exactly what it would involve. What you'd expect me to do.'

'OK, Claudia.' Hugo smiled, a dimple appearing in his left cheek as he did. 'Well, as I'm sure you know, the viewing public don't have a very favourable opinion of the people who run our businesses. The conception is that they're all smug, uncaring fat cats, creaming off the profits and awarding themselves massive bonuses while their employees struggle by on peanuts.'

'Well, that's certainly not the case here ...' The man had been in my office five minutes and already I was on the defensive. I couldn't see anything good coming out of this.

'I'm already aware of that. Gina's briefed me extensively on your commitment to paying the living wage, the various opportunities for career advancement within the Anthony Hotels chain, and the donations you make to charity. You're clearly a good employer.' His words should have mollified me more than they did. I was on edge, waiting for the next barb. It wasn't long in coming.

'But every business, no matter how successful,' Hugo continued, his fingers steepled together as he swivelled in his chair, 'always has areas that are in need of improvement. And for someone in the hospitality industry, like you, it's important that you get on top of those areas, given how easily a bad review or two on Trip Advisor and the like can influence a potential customer's choice of hotel ...'

Again, that wasn't something we had too much to worry about, I wanted to tell him. As part of her duties as head of PR, Gina regularly monitored those review sites, and I couldn't remember the last time she'd reported that one of our flagship hotels had received a serious trashing. All I said was, 'Yes, I'm aware of that.'

'Well, the beauty of *Secret CEO* is that it offers bosses the chance to go into their business at ground level and see for themselves the changes that need to be made. I don't know whether you've had the opportunity to look at the DVD of the last series I sent over to Gina last week.'

I shook my head. I'd been in Las Vegas for an industry convention, only coming back to London this morning on the red-eye flight. Even though I'd managed to sleep for most of the journey, jetlag still fogged my system, and out of all the tasks I had to catch up on, watching back-to-back episodes of a reality TV show was at the bottom of the list.

'OK, I see we have some catching up to do ...' If I was proving a hard sell on his concept – and I hoped I was – Hugo didn't show it. 'What you'd be doing, Claudia, is taking on a job in your own company, but you'd be in disguise, so that the employees you're working alongside don't have any idea who you really are.'

'And people really do this?' I scoffed. I knew television programmes were often built on the most tenuous of premises, but this all seemed particularly unlikely.

'Of course,' Gina chipped in. 'Hugo's been filling me in on how it's worked for other businesses. On the last series, the guy who founded the Don Giovanni pizza chain worked in one of his own restaurants for a month, taking orders and topping pizzas. After the show was broadcast, the company's turnover went up sixty-five per cent. You can't argue with figures like that, can you?'

I shrugged. 'That's fair enough, but it just feels a

bit … gimmicky. I can't see my father ever getting involved with a concept like this.'

'Which is exactly why when Hugo first approached me about the possibility of you taking part in the show, I wanted you to meet him,' Gina said. 'Gus Anthony was a fine man and a great boss to work for, but you've got to admit he was very set in his ways.'

Traditional, I would have called him. Committed to upholding the standards of the family business, and providing the high level of quality and service the Anthony name had come to stand for. But with that had come a certain resistance to change.

'You, on the other hand, are perfect for the show, Claudia,' Hugo told me. 'You're very young to be running a company as big as this, you're coming to the situation with fresh eyes and a new approach to business management, and I think you'd come across very well on camera. How we see this working for you is that there has to be one of your hotels which isn't doing as well as the others, whether that's in terms of occupancy rate or customer satisfaction …'

I tuned his voice out. At once, I knew the hotel that would be the focus of the programme, should I decide to go ahead with it. The black sheep of the chain, as my father had referred to it on more than one occasion.

William Anthony had begun to build hotels in the late 1860s, at first in the new industrial powerhouses of Manchester, Liverpool, and Sheffield. The flagship of his chain was on the Strand, a few minutes' walk from where I sat. It had been the first of the great luxury hotels in Britain, with innovations that were revolutionary at the time, including electric lighting and mechanically operated

4

lifts that would ferry guests to their rooms. As the spread of the railway network had encouraged the concept of the day trip and the seaside holiday, William had expanded his empire into fashionable resorts including Brighton and Bournemouth. All the hotels he'd opened still flourished – apart from the Anthony in the Welsh seaside resort of Aberpentre.

At one time, visitors had flocked to Aberpentre to sample the sulphurous waters from the local spring, which was supposed to offer health-giving benefits. To cater for these well-heeled tourists, William had built the finest hotel in the area. It commanded a spectacular view across the bay, and its Royal Suite was named for Edward VII, who stayed there when he was Prince of Wales. Now, however, it was a shadow of its former self; its grandeur faded and its rooms in dire need of refurbishment. In the weeks before his death, Dad had been considering an offer from an American property developer who was looking to buy the hotel. Like so many things, those negotiations had fallen apart in the wake of the sudden, massive heart attack that claimed my father's life.

The more I thought about it, the more I realised I could use an appearance on *Secret CEO* to my advantage. If nothing else, it would alert other potential buyers to the fact that the Anthony in Aberpentre was ripe for a takeover.

'Actually, I think we do have a hotel that might be right for your purposes ...' I began, noticing Gina sitting forward in her seat, alerted by the change in my tone. For the first time since we'd begun this meeting, I sounded positive. 'It's in Aberpentre. You know where that is, Hugo, right?'

He shook his head. That simple gesture told me all I needed to know. I smiled at him across the desk. 'And that's why if – and I haven't said I will yet – I go anywhere, it'll be there.'

'Glad to see you're coming round to my way of thinking.' Hugo's expression was smug. Clearly, he thought he'd already won the battle.

'But I'm not exactly an unfamiliar face within this company,' I pointed out. 'If I go undercover, I'm not convinced that someone won't recognise me.'

'Let me show you one of the makeovers we've done in previous episodes. It should help to put your mind to rest on that front.'

Hugo swiped a finger across the screen of the tablet he'd brought to the meeting with him and placed it on the desk before me. I saw a middle-aged man with greying locks and small, wire-rimmed glasses.

'That's Michael Corbett, managing director of Move-U,' he said. I recognised the name of the online estate agency, if not the face behind the company. 'And this –' Hugo's finger moved over the screen again, bringing up a fresh image '– is also Michael Corbett.'

Now, the glasses were gone, the hair was a rich chocolate brown, and the man sported a neat goatee. The transformation had the overall effect of making him look a good ten years younger, and I had to admit that if I hadn't been told they were photos of the same person, I would have struggled to guess.

'OK, that's impressive,' I conceded, still not wanting to commit myself totally to the proposal. 'But won't the staff be suspicious when I just turn up out of the blue? Particularly if I have a camera crew with me.'

'We already have a backstory planned for you,' Hugo explained. 'We'll tell the staff that yes, you're being filmed for a documentary, but it's about women who are being forced to make a radical career change due to the recession. As far as they're concerned, you'll have had a well-paid job somewhere in the finance sector, you've been made redundant, and now you have to start again, much lower down the career ladder. Trust me, Claudia, we really have thought of everything.'

'And if I agree to this, how soon would you want to start filming?'

'Well, it'll take us a couple of weeks to set everything up. We'll need to find accommodation for you, and smooth everything over with the hotel manager ...'

That was a thought. Who was in charge of the Anthony in Aberpentre these days? The manager we'd headhunted from a rival chain less than a year ago had moved on within a couple of months. He'd come with a string of impressive references, but had left as soon as he'd realised he wouldn't be able to revive the hotel's fortunes. The details of his replacement were a blur.

I stabbed at my computer keyboard, bringing up the personnel listing for Aberpentre and finding the name I sought.

'Rhodri Wynn-Jones,' I said, my eyes scanning the photograph that accompanied his listing. Dark hair, long enough to brush his shirt collar. Blue eyes, sharp cheekbones, and a hint of stubble on his chin. A tie that looked as though it had been hastily knotted around his neck moments before the photo was taken. The type my friends referred to as "a bit of rough" and my mother would have worried me about falling for.

7

Not that I intended to fall for men any more. I'd sworn off them following Gavin.

'Sounds like a local boy,' Hugo replied. 'That makes things interesting.'

I waited for him to elaborate, but he seemed to have addressed that last comment to himself. 'He's young, keen, full of ideas …' I continued. The first part at least wasn't a lie. Looking at his date of birth, I realised he was four years younger than me at twenty-seven. As for the rest, I could only assume that, like everyone who'd taken over the running of the hotel in recent years, he thought he was the one who could make it a success.

'Good, then I'm sure he'll be open to what we have in mind. Someone can provide me with a contact for him, right?'

'Of course,' Gina said. 'I'll make sure you have that before you leave.'

'Great. Once I've finalised the dates for filming, I'll be in touch with you again.' Hugo rose from his seat, and proffered a hand, wanting to shake on the deal. He didn't give me the opportunity to point out that I'd never actually agreed to be a part of the show, just wished Gina and I a pleasant day and left.

'What the hell happened there?' I asked, as the door slammed shut behind him, leaving me feeling like I'd been picked up and set down by a whirlwind.

'You just signed yourself up for a month working in a hotel in the back end of nowhere.' Gina smiled and raised her coffee cup to me in mock salute. 'Enjoy.'

'What do you mean you're going to be in disguise?'

I paused for the waiter to remove our plates before

8

resuming my conversation with Kay. We'd made this arrangement to meet for dinner well before the convention in Las Vegas, and originally I'd thought I'd be sharing tales of my trip to Sin City. Now, my days in the conference room and nights in the casino seemed like a very long time ago.

'Have you ever watched *Secret CEO*?'

'God, yes. Paul loves it. He's always saying how funny it would be if his own boss went undercover. He reckons he'd spot the guy immediately, but you know what Paul's like …'

'Well, I kind of got talked into taking part in the show. Don't say anything –' I said, as I noticed her lips quirk upwards in a smirk. She was clearly remembering an alcohol-fuelled rant of mine about the morons who put themselves forward to appear on reality TV, happy to be ridiculed and humiliated as long as they got their face on screen. 'I'd only just got off a long-haul flight. I wasn't at my sparkling best.'

The waiter had returned and stood discreetly at Kay's elbow, ready to present her with the dessert menu. She didn't even need to look at it before placing her order. 'I'll have the chocolate fondant, and my friend will have the tiramisu. Oh, and two filter coffees with warm milk, please. Thank you.'

'Kay,' I said as the waiter turned in the direction of the kitchen. 'What if I didn't want the tiramisu?'

'Darling, how many years have we been coming here?' she replied. 'And in all that time, have you ever ordered anything else?'

She was right, of course. We'd discovered this old-fashioned Italian restaurant, just off Drury Lane, in our university days, back when we'd been sharing a flat and counting the pennies. Even though I'd come into my trust fund at the age of twenty-one and Kay had married Paul, who earned a six-figure salary as an investment manager, we still came here a couple of times a year to catch up on each other's gossip over a glass or two of Barolo. I'd eaten in restaurants all round the world, and I'd never had a better plate of pasta *all'amatriciana* anywhere. As for the tiramisu, it might mean putting in double duty on the treadmill to burn off the calories, but every sweet, creamy mouthful was so worth it.

'Anyway, you were telling me about your impending TV appearance.' Kay propped her elbow on the table and rested the point of her chin in her hand, waiting for me to go on.

'Oh yes. I've agreed to spend four weeks in our hotel in Aberpentre. It's on the Llŷn Peninsula – the north-west coast of Wales,' I informed her when she just looked at me blankly. 'I'm going to be working there as just another employee, at least as far as the staff are concerned, but really the idea is I'll be looking at what's going wrong there and seeing how things can be improved.'

I drained the last of the wine in my glass. No matter how many times I considered the concept, I still couldn't help thinking that I was setting myself up for a fall. Kay, at least, seemed enthusiastic about the prospect.

'That sounds brilliant. What are you going to be doing, working as a chambermaid or something?'

I shook my head. 'No, I'll be on the front desk. It's the one thing I'm insisting on. Don't take this the wrong way, but cleaning rooms is absolutely the last job I'd do. Been there, done that, after all.'

When I'd been at university, Dad had set me up with a job in one of his hotels every summer. I had always been employed in a menial role, from working in the laundry room to washing pots in the kitchen. It had been his way of giving me hands-on experience in preparation for joining the company full time, and it had made sure I'd never got too full of myself. I'd been part of the housekeeping team at the Brighton Anthony, and I didn't exactly look back on my time there with fondness. The girls I'd worked with – mostly students like me, or recent arrivals in the country – were a nice-enough lot, but I shuddered at the memory of dubious stains on the sheets, clogged toilets, and the items left behind by departing guests, from false teeth to worn underwear. I'd even found the odd sex toy under the bed, no doubt thrown aside at the moment of orgasm, and forgotten about. Some people seemed to think they could make as much mess as they liked, since it would be someone else's job to clean up after them.

The arrival of our desserts brought me out of my reverie. I looked at the scoop of vanilla ice cream slowly melting in rivulets on top of Kay's chocolate fondant pudding and wondered whether I should have been more adventurous in my own choice. As it always did, the first mouthful of tiramisu persuaded me otherwise.

'Don't make it obvious you've noticed him,' Kay said, pausing with her spoon halfway between the plate and her mouth, 'but there's a man at the table in the corner who keeps looking at you. Fair hair, beefy, rugby-player type. Not all at all bad looking ...'

'Are you sure he's looking at me? He could just be trying to catch the waiter's attention. Probably just wants

11

to pay his bill and leave.'

Kay sighed. 'When did you become so oblivious to male attention?'

'Not oblivious,' I told her. 'Just not interested.' Turning my head a fraction, I caught a glimpse of the man Kay had been talking about. He sat with a couple of other men, who were braying at a joke one of them had made. Not my type, even if I had been looking for someone. Too blond, too brash, too keen to be noticed.

'It's been nearly two years since Gavin,' Kay commented. 'Are you really going to let every opportunity pass you by because of him?'

'This has got nothing to do with Gavin.' I stuck my spoon into my rapidly dwindling portion of dessert.

'Rubbish. It's got everything to do with him. Look, just because he was a slimy little shit who deserves to be dropped head-first off the top of the Shard doesn't mean every man is the same.'

'I don't want to talk about this now, Kay.' The many inventive ways in which she pictured Gavin Elston coming to a gruesome end at her hands could usually be relied on to bring a smile to my face, but not tonight. Somehow, I couldn't bury the memories of my former fiancé's duplicity.

'You've got to stop thinking any man who tries to get close to you is only after your money,' she persisted. 'There are lots of good men out there, men who will value you for who you are, and not what you own.' Her face brightened. 'Hey, maybe you'll meet someone while you're undercover. Someone who thinks you're just another employee of Anthony Hotels, not the woman who runs the whole thing.'

An image flashed into my mind. A face with overlong black hair and blue eyes: a particular weakness as far as I was concerned. All my favourite fantasies revolved around someone with that dark, Celtic colouring and brooding intensity; someone who gave the impression that getting close to him would be a challenge. But when you broke through the defences he had built around himself, his mouth would be as soft as his kisses were demanding. He would take me in his arms and kiss me until my lips were swollen and my body threatened to dissolve beneath the delicious onslaught. Then he would move lower, trailing a path of kisses down my neck and the soft curve of my breast, until the last of my inhibitions were gone and I was begging him to use his mouth where I needed it the most …

I blinked the thought away, aware that Kay was regarding me with a curious expression. 'Don't be ridiculous,' I snapped. 'That's the last thing I'm going to be looking for.'

She smiled. 'Stranger things have happened. Who would have thought I'd meet the man I was destined to marry at a karaoke night, of all places?'

The group of men at the corner table had settled their bill and were making their way towards the front door. As they passed our table, the burly blond dropped something onto the red and white chequered tablecloth by my elbow. When I looked down, I saw it was his business card. I didn't even bother to read the details, just waited till he and his friends had left the restaurant, then tore the thin piece of card in half.

Kay said nothing, but her disapproval was all too obvious.

I let out a sigh. 'Kay, I know you want me to see me settled down, but I'm perfectly happy being single, honestly. With everything I have on my plate, a man is the last thing I need in my life right now. And even if I were looking, do you seriously think I'd go all the way to Wales to find someone? I mean, there are so many ways this whole *Secret CEO* thing could go horribly wrong anyway, without adding that kind of complication.'

Kay said nothing, just gave me a "we'll see about that" kind of look. I did my best to stifle a yawn, still not fully over my jetlag. It signalled the end of the conversation, as we both seemed to realise how late it was getting.

'Are you going to be OK to get home?' Kay asked. 'We can share a cab if you like.'

I shook my head. 'No need, I'm going to spend tonight at the Anthony on the Strand. I rang earlier, asked them to keep a room free for me.'

'The perks of being the boss, eh? Well, enjoy it now; there'll be none of that once you're in Wales.' Kay smiled, and turned her body in the direction of our waiter, making a scribbling motion against her palm to let him know she'd like him to bring us the bill.

'Don't worry, I think I can cope with being one of the plebs,' I assured her, and hoped my confident words masked the anxiety I felt about stepping into the unknown.

TWO

Nearly a fortnight passed without my hearing from the production company, and I'd started to think that maybe Hugo Murray had changed his mind, and decided against using me on *Secret CEO*. As I was wondering whether this might not actually be a good thing, my phone rang.

'Hi, this is Tanya from Wild Card. Am I speaking to Claudia Anthony?'

'Yes, you are. How can I help you, Tanya?'

'I'm ringing to let you know we've finalised your itinerary for the filming in Aberpentre, and I have all the details for you …'

By the time Tanya ended the call, I had the date and time of the train I'd be taking down to Wales, the address of the apartment that had been rented for me for the duration of my stay, and a suitable cover story. I needed a fake identity, and we'd settled on Jane Ennis – a combination of my middle name and my mother's maiden name. As far as everyone working at the hotel was concerned, I had been employed as a financial planning manager for a firm in Caernarfon. In the nine months since I'd been made redundant, I had tried and failed to find a similar job, and now I was looking to start a new career in the hospitality industry. A month's trial behind the front desk of the Anthony would let me know whether I was cut out for such work.

But before I left for Aberpentre, there was the small matter of the change in my physical appearance to deal with. Tanya had booked me an appointment at a hair salon close to Wild Card's office in Camden. I'd wanted to visit my regular stylist, who I'd been using for the best part of five years, but Luka had a string of celebrity clients, and Tanya thought my turning up at his premises with a camera crew in tow might not be the best idea.

'You're going to film me having my hair done?' I'd asked.

'Of course. How else do you think the viewers are going to see the full impact of your transformation?'

That's when I seriously began to wonder what I was getting myself into. But the arrangements had been made. Like it or not, I couldn't back out now.

The following Monday morning, I arrived at Mirage, which billed itself as a "fresh and funky hair design studio" and occupied a unit in the revamped Camden Stables Market. Tanya had booked me the first appointment of the day, and it was barely nine o'clock as I crossed the flagstones towards the hair studio.

Waiting on the doorstep was the two-man film crew who'd been assigned to follow me for the length of the project. The cameraman had been munching on some kind of breakfast burrito. His auburn hair stuck up at odd angles, and he looked like he hadn't long been out of bed. He wiped his hand on his T-shirt, which bore the image of the Evil Monkey from *Family Guy*, and held it out for me

16

to shake. 'You must be Claudia. Dean Parker.'

His grip was surprisingly firm, the smile that crinkled the corners of his blue eyes warm and genuine. 'Hello, Dean. I hope I haven't kept you waiting.'

'No, we only just got here. The traffic on the Euston Road was a nightmare.'

'Isn't it always?' his companion chipped in. This second man had skin the colour of bitter chocolate and a voice that was pure West Yorkshire. 'I'm Bayo Diarra, by the way, and I'm the sound guy.' He gestured to the microphone he held. The fuzzy grey cover made it look as though he had a small terrier in his clutches.

'I don't mean to be rude,' I said, 'but I'm trying to place your accent. Is it Leeds?'

'Spot on.' Bayo looked impressed. 'How did you guess?'

'Oh, when I left university, I worked in the Anthony Hotel in Leeds for a year.' It had been the next step in my training, after my various summer jobs. Rising to the challenge of running the place and dealing with whatever problems arose, from staff calling in sick to the kitchen freezers breaking down, had taught me so much.

'I know it well,' he said. 'My sister had her wedding reception there, would you believe?'

It didn't surprise me to hear that. The hotel, a magnificent example of Victorian Gothic architecture, possessed a function room that had been booked out for wedding parties almost every weekend during the time I'd been in charge there.

Dean crumpled his burrito wrapper, looked around for a bin to put it in, and failed to find one. 'OK, Claudia. What we'd like to do first is film you going into the shop. Hugo

17

wants us to get a lot of establishing shots, since they give the editor plenty to work with. I want you to just try and pretend that the camera's not here, and behave as naturally as you can.' He raised the camera to his shoulder. 'Right, if you're ready, in you go.'

It was hard not to feel self-conscious as I pushed open the door of the salon and stepped through it; even more so when Dean called me back and asked me to do it again. I couldn't believe I'd managed to do something as simple as walking into a shop incorrectly, but he explained he just wanted to film me from another angle.

Once he was happy with his shot, I walked inside the salon. The white-painted walls and large, oval mirrors gave the long, low room a feeling of space. I was greeted by a pixie-featured girl who looked to be barely out of her teens, and whose short, spiky hair was an arresting shade of candyfloss pink.

'Claudia, I'm Maxie. Come through, please.'

Maxie led me to her station in front of one of the mirrors. Her scissors and styling tools were already laid out neatly, and a trolley holding all the equipment necessary for dying hair stood by the side of a red leather swivel chair.

She helped me into a loose, leopard print smock, which she tied with a sash around my waist.

My reflection in the mirror appeared pale and anxious, and I willed myself to relax, aware of Dean taking up a position behind me, his camera on his shoulder. 'Am I allowed to ask what you're planning to do to me?' I said.

Maxie grinned. 'And spoil the surprise?' She ran her hands through my hair, nodding to herself as she registered its condition. 'Relax, Claudia, I reserve the

18

novelty shades for myself. Let me get you a coffee, and then I'll go mix up the dye.'

My fears didn't recede as she fussed around me, painting a bluish, creamy mixture along my hair from root to ends. Dean filmed for a few moments then, having captured what he needed, he and Bayo went outside for a cigarette break. Maxie called both of them back inside once the dye had worked its magic and she was ready to begin cutting.

'Now, I'm going to take about six inches off the length,' she informed me. 'You're sure you're OK with that?'

I wasn't, not at all, but I nodded and closed my eyes as she snipped away, not wanting to see the wet strands of hair landing on the salon floor. I'd never had a drastic change of hairstyle, not even when Gavin and I had split up – an event that so often precipitates a radical alteration in a woman's image. And as I didn't have the faintest idea of the look Maxie was trying to achieve, I had no idea how I'd react when she unveiled my transformation.

She turned the chair so I faced away from the mirror while she blow-dried my hair and applied a finishing serum. Bayo, who must have spotted the tension on my face, winked and mouthed, "You look great." I wanted to be reassured by his comment, but uncertainty gnawed at my gut. It wasn't just down to the haircut; again, I found myself wondering whether taking part in *Secret CEO* would really provide any kind of fillip for the company. But in a little over two hours, I'd be on a train on my way to Birmingham, where I would connect with the stopping service to Aberpentre. It was too late to back out now.

'Are you ready for the big reveal?' Maxie spoke as

much to Dean as to me.

'As I'll ever be,' I murmured.

'Here we go, then …' With that, she spun me round, so I was confronted with my reflection.

'Oh my …' My reaction must have appeared cartoonishly comical, my eyes wide as my hands flew to cover my mouth. I'd entered the salon with long, blonde hair, shot through with streaks of honey and caramel. Now, I had a choppy bob in a rich brown with coppery highlights designed to bring out the gold flecks in my green eyes. No one who'd seen me walk into Mirage would believe it was the same woman who left.

'It looks amazing. Thanks so much, Maxie.'

'My pleasure.' Her eyes sparkled with the satisfaction of a job well done.

The production company had provided me with a pair of small, black-framed glasses with plain lenses, designed to complete my disguise. At Dean's request, I slipped them on while he continued filming. 'They'll need that so they can splice together a "before and after" shot,' he informed me.

I stood up, and Maxie brushed some stray pieces of hair off my shoulders before untying the smock.

'You shouldn't really need to touch the roots up while you're away,' she said. 'And you'll have no problems going back to your old colour afterwards, though I really do think this shade suits you so well.'

With one last, disbelieving look in the mirror, I gathered my handbag and the wheeled suitcase that contained everything I thought I'd need over the next four weeks, then left the salon.

'We can drop you at Euston station if you'd like,' Bayo

said. The plan was that he and Dean would drive up and be waiting to film my arrival when I got off the train at Aberpentre.

I shook my head. 'It's OK, I'll walk. It's a nice day, after all.' And I'm going to be sitting on a train for most of the rest of it, I almost added. At least I would have time to catch up on some paperwork I hadn't quite managed to complete over the weekend. The day-to-day running of the company would be in safe hands in my absence, but I needed to let people know why I wouldn't be available to answer my phone for the next four weeks. From the moment I arrived in Wales, Claudia Anthony would cease to exist, and I'd effectively become Jane Ennis. With my gorgeous new hairstyle, and the glasses I'd tucked safely back in my handbag, I was halfway there. Leaving London, and my pressurised role as CEO behind, would complete the process. For the first time since I'd agreed to take part in the programme, I was actually looking forward to being someone else.

Eight hours later, my newfound enthusiasm for the project had dwindled considerably. The train journey to Birmingham had been uneventful enough, and I'd made my connection at New Street with time to spare. After that, I'd spent over five hours trundling through places I'd never even heard of before, as the stopping service made its way through Telford, Shrewsbury, and over the border into Wales. Stations with names I had no idea how to pronounce (Machynlleth, Llwyngwril, Morfa Mawddach) came and went, some so small they didn't even have a booking office, just a brick-built shelter for passengers to wait in.

21

The railway line followed a coastal course, hugging the shoreline, with the looming shadow of the mountains never too far away. I might have enjoyed watching the ever-changing scenery, but the rain had set in somewhere outside Wolverhampton, obscuring the view. Now, as the sky darkened and evening drew in, all I could see as the train approached Aberpentre station was a collection of industrial units and marshalling yards, signalling the terminus.

'Aberpentre is our next and final station stop,' came the recorded announcement. 'This train terminates here. Would passengers leaving the train please remember to take all their belongings with them.'

By now, I was the only person in the carriage, apart from a young man in army fatigues who'd boarded at Shrewsbury and dozed for most of the journey. I hoped he hadn't managed to sleep past his stop as he shook himself awake and looked round, but he just grunted as he registered his surroundings and picked up his kitbag.

I followed the soldier down the aisle, wheeling my case along behind me. Waiting on the platform as I stepped down from the train were two familiar figures. Dean had his camera hoisted on his shoulder. Knowing that he'd be filming one of his beloved establishing shots, I didn't wave or in any way acknowledge him or Bayo as I walked towards them.

'Was that OK?' I asked as I reached the pair. 'You don't need me to do it again, or anything?'

Dean shook his head. 'That was great, thanks, Claudia. Good journey?'

'Not bad, though it took forever. Who knew there were so many stations between here and Birmingham. And there were no buffet facilities on the train, so I'm absolutely dying for a cup of tea.'

'Well, we'll give you a lift to your apartment,' Bayo said. 'It's only down the road from the Anthony Hotel; couldn't be more convenient.'

He led us over to his elderly Ford Focus estate, parked on the station forecourt. He hefted my case into the boot, and I made space for myself on the back seat, most of which was covered with road atlases, bits of golfing equipment, and ketchup-smeared fast food wrappers. Dean sat in the front, his camera cradled between his legs.

Once he'd fastened his seat belt, Bayo reversed the car out of its parking spot and on to the road.

'And where are you staying?' I asked.

'The same block as you,' Dean replied. 'Tanya thought it would make sense to have us all staying in the one place, plus this time of the year there was no problem getting the two apartments together. It'd probably be a different story in the summer holidays.'

I doubted that. The rain lashed down with a vengeance, beating against the car windows, but the glimpses I caught of the town told me you'd always be able to find somewhere to stay, even at the height of the season. Assuming you wanted to. Aberpentre looked like a town down on its luck, the days of Royal visits and well-to-do ladies making trips to drink the spa waters long behind it. The high street appeared to be dominated by building societies, bookmakers, and charity shops, giving way to little cafés and shops selling lettered rock and assorted holiday tat as we drew nearer to the promenade. It was too dark to make out more than the outline of Aberpentre Bay as I looked out to sea; the string of coloured lights that

23

hung from ornate wrought-iron lampposts did little to illuminate the view, as many of the bulbs had blown and were in need of replacement.

'Here's the Anthony, coming up on the right,' Bayo announced. I turned to look at the hotel, with its imposing Victorian façade. From everything Dad had said, I knew the interior was overdue a makeover – something we'd discussed at several of our monthly board meetings but had somehow never got round to placing high on the list of priorities. But I hadn't realised the exterior had become so dilapidated too. The stonework was a dull, weathered grey, the ironwork on the balconies in need of a coat of paint. Though the lights in the entrance hall gave off a welcoming golden glow, I wasn't sure that if I were looking for somewhere to stay, this would be my first choice – or any choice, for that matter. The Anthony chain prided itself on providing high-quality accommodation at an affordable price, but I wouldn't know how far this particular hotel was falling short of that aim until I went inside.

Tomorrow morning, in my Jane Ennis persona, I would be doing just that.

'Here we are.' Bayo brought the car to a halt, faltering me in my musing. 'Home sweet home – for the next month, anyway.'

He'd pulled up in the car park of a low, undistinguished redbrick building. The sign outside said in stark, black plastic lettering, *Bay Vista Holiday Apartments* – or it would have done, if the "s" in "Vista" hadn't been missing. A white van with *Llewellyn and Sons, Builders* and a Porthmadog address written on the side occupied the space next to Bayo's Focus. I remembered something

Tanya had told me when she'd been giving me the details of my accommodation: many of these apartments were occupied outside the summer holiday season by contractors doing work in the area. At least this place had found a way of maximising its revenue streams, to use a phrase that came up so often in the board meetings I chaired.

Having retrieved our luggage from the boot, we dashed up the steps to the front door. The concierge, a woman in her forties with stiffly styled blonde hair, welcomed me like a long-lost friend. 'Miss Ennis, isn't it? I'm Gaynor Rhys. Lovely to see you.'

Gaynor walked round to her desk, her plump hips rolling beneath her navy smock dress. 'You'll be staying in Apartment 7, on the second floor. It has one of the nicest views of the bay.' She retrieved a key ring from the top drawer, and passed it to me. 'The silver Yale key is for the main door, and the gold for your apartment. I'm usually on duty between 9 a.m. and 9 p.m., and there's a contact number if you require any help outside those hours. This,' she handed me a typewritten sheet of paper, 'has details of all the local amenities you might need. The banks, the post office, the supermarket – though I've made sure your fridge is already stocked with a few things as I knew you'd be getting here quite late.'

'Thanks, that's very kind of you.'

She smiled broadly. 'All part of the service, dear. We like to make sure all our guests have everything they need.' As she spoke, I noticed she shot a look at Bayo from beneath her eyelashes. He seemed to be ignoring her attention. 'Now, if I've forgotten to mention anything, just pop down to the desk here before I leave tonight. And do have a lovely stay.'

'She seems nice,' I said, as I followed Dean and Bayo out of the lobby and up a flight of uncarpeted stairs.

'Oh she is. Very friendly,' Dean replied. 'And she's already taken a shine to Bayo. Which is lucky, seeing as he's a single guy, and all. Just perfect for a horny Welsh cougar to clasp to her ample bosom ...'

As he spoke, I realised I didn't know anything about the personal lives of either of these two men. They seemed happy enough to uproot themselves from their own homes for the duration of filming, but I supposed that was a necessary requirement if you were part of a TV crew.

Halting him in his teasing of his colleague, I said, 'And what about you, Dean? Have you got a wife or a girlfriend?'

'Boyfriend.' It hadn't occurred to me that he might be gay, but I said nothing as he continued, 'Maurice works in musical theatre, mostly. He's on the road at the moment, in a touring production of *Seven Brides for Seven Brothers*. So us being apart for a while is nothing new. Actually, I'm hoping to meet up with him in a couple of weeks, when the tour reaches Chester.' He grinned. 'So, babe, you'll have to promise not to do anything that's worthy of catching on camera while I'm away.'

They came to a stop before a white-painted door with the number four fixed to it.

'Well, this is us,' Dean said. 'According to our notes, you're meeting the hotel manager at eight tomorrow morning, right?' I nodded. 'OK, we'll see you outside the Anthony at ten to.'

'Don't tell me. Establishing shots, right? Good night, boys.'

26

As I climbed the stairs to the second floor, I could still hear the two men bickering, Bayo's voice slightly raised as he responded to Dean's accusations about him being the subject of Gaynor Rhys's attentions. At least I felt like I had a couple of friends in this unfamiliar town, even before I began trying to ingratiate myself with the locals.

The apartment was clean, airy, and smelled faintly of vanilla. I left my suitcase in the lounge, and went into the room that doubled as a kitchen and dining area to see what Gaynor had provided in the fridge for me. I retrieved eggs, and set about scrambling them. In the bread bin, I found a crusty white loaf, and toasted a couple of slices, buttering them thickly. Lunch, which had been a pasta salad I'd bought from a concession at New Street station before getting on the train to Aberpentre, seemed like a very long time ago now.

Outside, the rain still pattered against the windows. I pulled the blinds, and took my supper through to the lounge. Switching on the TV, I flicked through the channels, lingering for a moment on what I realised was the American version of *Secret CEO*. The hapless chief executive of some theme restaurant chain was working undercover as a waiter, and had almost got himself sacked on the spot for spilling a plate of popcorn shrimp over the customer he was serving. Not wanting to watch any more for fear it would make me think of all the ways my own appearance on the show could go horribly wrong, I found instead some action movie in which Jason Statham, shirtless and glistening with oil and sweat, was fighting half a dozen men simultaneously. The plot didn't seem to make much sense, but the actor looked pretty good running around half-naked, so I let the images wash over

27

me.

In the morning, I had to walk into one of my own hotels and take over the running of the reception desk. How hard would it be to act as though I didn't know anything about the company? How would the other staff treat me, having no knowledge of my real identity and aware that I wouldn't even be working beside them if it weren't for some stupid reality show? And how would I cope, spending a month in this sad, rundown little town where the only friends I had were the cameraman and sound guy employed to follow my every move?

Aware that it was far too late to be getting cold feet now, I closed my eyes and was asleep before I knew it.

THREE

The alarm on my phone went off at 6.30, just as it did on any other working day. Startled awake by the sound, I looked around, wondering why I'd been asleep on the sofa in a room I didn't recognise. Memories of last night came back slowly as I hauled myself to my feet.

On the TV, the breakfast news was playing softly to itself. A reporter stood outside a school, doing a piece to camera; I caught the words "pensions" and "strike action" before switching the set off. If I'd been back in London, I'd have fitted in a visit to the gym before going to the office. Today, I didn't have that option, but I knew a run would clear my head and ease the ache in my limbs that came from sleeping in such a weird, cramped position.

Last night, I hadn't even bothered to unpack my case. Now, I hunted through it for sweatpants, a hooded top, and my training shoes. Having changed into my running gear, I went to fish an elastic band from my handbag so I could tie back my hair, before remembering that with my new, short style it wouldn't be necessary. Making sure I had my keys and mobile phone with me, I quietly let myself out of the apartment and hurried down two flights of stairs to the lobby.

Outside, last night's rainstorm had blown itself out, and the day was dawning bright and fair. The sky had a mother-of-pearl sheen; the air was fresh and carried a faint tang of the sea. I gazed out towards the horizon, for the first time able to appreciate the sweeping curve of Aberpentre Bay. A long, wooden pier jutted out into the sea. At the mouth of the bay, to my left, the square tower of a castle stood in ruins on a tree-covered promontory. The scene held a beauty that had been entirely lacking when we'd driven along the promenade last night.

I stood in the car park of the Bay Vista apartments and stretched out my calves and my quads, making sure the muscles were loose and warm. My plan was to run to the end of the prom and back; a distance, I reckoned, of around a couple of miles. That would give me plenty of time to get back to my apartment, have a shower, grab some breakfast, and walk down to the Anthony Hotel in time to meet Dean and Bayo.

Slipping the headphones of my MP3 player into my ear, I shuffled to the playlist I'd put together for my workout sessions; tunes designed to motivate and keep me moving, even on those mornings when the last thing I wanted to do was exercise. The opening bars of Kasabian's *Processed Beats* had me bouncing on my toes in a jog, out of the car park, across the road, and on to the promenade.

My trainers slapped against the pavement in a steady rhythm. Just being out and about before the rest of the town had properly woken up felt good, and I inhaled long, deep lungfuls of air, relishing the sensation of putting my body through its paces.

Down on the beach, a man stood at the water's edge, throwing a stick for his Alsatian puppy to chase. The dog

30

bounded into the surf, splashing and wagging its tail excitedly. If it wasn't for the drivers of the cars that passed me every now and again, the dog owner and I could have been the only people on Earth.

I ran past the Anthony and on. Now, I passed a series of small bed and breakfast hotels, interspersed with gift shops, fish and chip restaurants, and even a couple of stalls selling cockles, clams, and other local seafood. The shops were shuttered and silent at this time of day, the curtains on the B&B windows drawn. Though I couldn't entirely shake the impression that this town had seen better days, I could picture this particular stretch of the seafront being lively in the high days of summer.

A set of weathered steps cut into the sea wall led down to the beach. I descended them carefully, the stone having been worn to a groove in the middle of each step by a combination of the weather and the steady passage of thousands of pairs of feet. Running on sand was harder than asphalt, but I moved with long, easy strides, oblivious to everything but the music that accompanied me. Lost in my own little world, I did my best to let go of all the usual concerns that nagged at me – making a success of the business, living up to my father's reputation, and the thing I found hardest of all to shake, the memory of Gavin Elston, and the way he'd tried to use me to further his career. Thank God I'd found out what he was really like before our marriage had gone ahead. It was bad enough that he'd ingratiated himself with Dad, and attempted to weasel his way onto the board of directors; the fact that he might have been able to walk away with half of my assets if we divorced, not to mention the damage he could have done to the company in the process, was too sickening to contemplate. If I hadn't had the guts to call off the engagement … But Kay was right: that was all in the past. I had to forget about it and move on.

The most obvious landmark on the prom, unsurprisingly, was the Anthony, and I used it like a beacon. Once I was alongside it, I looked out for the nearest set of steps. Reaching them, I came to a stop and switched off the music. Having performed the same stretches I'd used before setting out, this time to help me cool down, I climbed the steps and walked back to Bay Vista. The car park had been full when I'd left, but now I noticed a couple of gaps where vehicles, including the builders' van I'd seen the night before, had departed.

Back in my apartment, I showered and dressed in my new work uniform of black skirt and jacket, white blouse, and black shoes with heels low enough to make being on my feet all day comfortable. Though I had any number of skirt suits and blouses at home, I'd acquired these particular clothes in the chain stores of Oxford Street last weekend. Jane Ennis, out of work for the best part of a year, could no longer afford the upmarket labels that littered my wardrobe and would once been have part of hers; in my mind, circumstances had forced her to become a Dorothy Perkins and Primark kind of woman, and I'd shopped accordingly.

Breakfast consisted of toast, marmalade, and a glass of fresh orange juice. I'd need to fit in a trip to the supermarket at some point over the next couple of days; maybe I'd be able to slip out to the shops in my lunch break. So many things to think about, but at least I couldn't imagine the *Secret CEO* team needing footage of me doing something as mundane as buying groceries.

I kept my make-up minimal – BB cream, a couple of coats of mascara, and a lip-gloss in a neutral shade. Remembering to put on my glasses, I checked my reflection and left for work, half-expecting to bump into Dean and Bayo on the stairs.

There was no sign of them in the apartment complex. When I reached the Anthony, they were already waiting on the forecourt for me.

'Morning, Claudia – or should that be Jane?' Dean said. 'All ready for the big day?'

I nodded. 'Yeah, I'm looking forward to it.' I spoke more to convince myself than him.

'There's one thing we forgot to do yesterday,' he went on, 'and that was to give you your own camera so you can keep a video diary. You won't need to film yourself every day; just if something happens that you really feel you need to talk about. But because we didn't ask you to discuss your feelings about the prospect of working undercover in the Anthony last night, I'd like you to do that now, if you don't mind.'

'Sure. What do you need me to do?'

'You can just stand where you are, and I'll ask you a couple of things,' Dean said. 'And I want you to answer them in a way that incorporates the question.' I must have looked confused by this, because he clarified, 'If I ask, for instance, "Why are you looking forward to this?" then don't just start your answer with, "Because." I want you to say, "I'm looking forward to this because …" They cut out my questions in the editing stage, you see, and just leave your words. Does that make sense?'

'Yes, I've got it.'

'Right, can you just give me your name and tell me

what you had for breakfast, just so Bayo can check the sound levels? And try to look at me, rather than looking directly into the camera. OK, in three, two, one …'

When he finished counting down the numbers, I cleared my throat and began, 'Hello, my name is –' I started to say "Claudia", and caught myself just in time '– Jane Ennis, and for breakfast I had toast and marmalade.'

Dean glanced over at Bayo, who wore a headset plugged into a small recording device. 'How was that?'

'Fine.' He smiled at me. 'Very good, Jane, very confident. You sure you haven't done this before?'

His comment was clearly designed to help me relax, but it did the trick nonetheless.

'OK, babe, this time we go for real,' Dean said. He pointed the camera at me again. 'What do you think you'll gain from this experience?'

I didn't hesitate. 'What I think I will gain from –' At that moment, a heavy goods lorry rumbled past on the road, drowning out my answer. Bayo shook his head.

'Sorry, we're going to have to go again.'

Dean flashed me an apologetic smile. 'The joys of location filming. Let's try that one more time. So, what are you intending to gain from this experience?'

'What I'm hoping to gain from this experience,' I repeated, 'is an insight into what a customer expects when they stay at an Anthony Hotel, what our staff expect as employees of the company, and what I can do to help meet these expectations.'

'Are you at all concerned that you might be recognised while you're here?' Dean asked.

'I don't think anyone will recognise me.' I laughed. 'This morning, I didn't even recognise myself!'

34

'That's great,' Dean said. 'Just what we wanted. Now, I just need to get a shot of you going into the hotel …'

When I entered the lobby, a man I recognised stood in wait. Rhodri Wynn-Jones, taller and broader than I'd anticipated from the head-and-shoulders shot that had accompanied his staff profile. He didn't look overly thrilled to see me, but I hoped his reaction had more to do with the camera crew that followed in my wake; I knew I wouldn't have welcomed such a disruption to my normal routine, even with an advance briefing.

I plastered my brightest smile on my face and went to greet him. 'Hello, I'm Jane Ennis. You must be Rhodri.'

'Jane. Nice to have you here.' His voice was so low I almost expected Bayo to complain about his sound levels and ask him to repeat the words. It had the same gentle Welsh lilt I'd heard from Gaynor Rhys. When he took my hand in his, I felt my breath catch in my throat.

Had he felt that same fizzing surge of energy as our skin made contact? If so, he didn't show it. I stepped back a pace, unsettled by the strength of my body's reaction to him.

'So,' Rhodri went on, 'you're going to be working on Reception for us, right? Come over, and I'll start off by showing you the checking-in procedure.'

I followed him round behind the desk. He gestured to a computer, which, I couldn't help but notice, was considerably older than the ones at the front desk of the Anthony in the Strand.

'OK, so when a guest arrives to check in, the first thing to remember is that you greet them with a smile and welcome them to the Anthony Hotel. You ask their name, and then you look up their booking on the system. Now, I don't know whether you've used a similar kind of system before ...'

I bit my tongue. As Claudia, I had more than a passing familiarity with the software we used across our chain of hotels. I hadn't needed to access a reservation, or check a customer in or out, since the days when I'd done the odd shift on the front desk in Leeds. However, I'd been in on all the discussions when we'd updated our system, and been talked through the process by its designers, who'd wanted to show me the simplicity of their programme. As Jane, however, I came from a finance background, and all this would have been alien to me.

'To be honest, I've only ever worked with accounting software. If you want me to sort out a spreadsheet for you, that's no problem. Otherwise, you're going to have to show me what to do.'

'That's what I thought.' Did I detect a hint of irritation in his voice? If so, I wasn't surprised. Rhodri would be used to employing Reception staff who already had experience of the hotel industry, not a complete novice like Jane Ennis. Even at this early hour, I'd be preventing him from attending to his other duties. But he turned a brisk smile on me, and pressed the "enter" key. The floating Anthony Hotel logo that acted as a screensaver disappeared, and the reservation system came up.

'OK, we're already logged in, so to give you an example, Mr Smith wants to check in to the room he's booked. So we type in "Smith", and that will bring up all the reservations under that name ...'

His fingers skipped over the keyboard as he spoke. I waited for the list of names to appear. And waited. And waited ...

Rhodri muttered what sounded like a curse under his breath. 'Looks like the system's frozen again.'

'Does this happen often?'

'Since we had the new system installed a few months ago, all the time.' He shrugged. 'If they'd upgraded the computers at the same time, it might not be so much of a problem.'

'So what do you do now?'

'Usually, we wait. Nine times out of ten, it'll move on to the next screen eventually. If not, we know it's crashed … Oh, here we go.' I glanced at the monitor again. As Rhodri continued to talk me through the check-in procedure, I made a mental note to check the schedule for hotel upgrades when I eventually got back to the office. The Aberpentre might be right at the bottom of the list of priorities for refurbishment, but it didn't mean the staff had to use outdated computer equipment that only served to make their job harder and more frustrating.

Once Rhodri was satisfied that I'd be able to use the system without someone on hand to guide me through the process, he started to talk me through the rest of my duties.

'When you book the guest in, you need to choose a suitable room for them in terms of location. They'll already have asked for single or a double, of course, and obviously, that will be decided according to the size of the party. But you also need to use your common sense and factor in things like whether you're dealing with an elderly person who may not be very mobile, or a couple with young children who won't want to be manoeuvring a buggy in and out of the lift.'

'Why should that be a problem?'

'I'll show you in a moment. The lift is a beautiful piece of engineering – or it was when it was installed. Like a lot of things in this hotel, though, it hasn't exactly moved with the times.' Again, I detected a resigned tone to his comment, and wondered whether, despite everything I'd heard about his enthusiasm for the job, he was already beginning to have second thoughts about working here.

'OK,' he went on, 'we use a key card system here, and when you give the key to the guest, it needs to be in one of these …' He showed me a small, folded piece of card, which had slots designed to hold the key, and spaces for the desk clerk to write in the customer's name and room number. 'You also need to make sure they return it to you when they check out.'

By now, I had completely forgotten that our conversation was being filmed. I'd been assured that I would become oblivious to the presence of the camera crew, but I hadn't expected it to happen quite so quickly. Perhaps it was Dean's unobtrusive style that made me feel comfortable – or as comfortable as I could be at the side of Rhodri Wynn-Jones. 'Right, got it,' I murmured.

'You'll also be required to prepare bills at the end of a guest's stay, and take their payments. If they've booked online, either directly with the hotel or via a third-party site, then they should have been charged the full amount for the room already, but check whether they want to pay for breakfast, room service, or anything like that. You may also have to take messages, in which case you have to make sure they're passed on to the guest promptly. And from time to time, you might also have to deal with special requests, like storing valuable items or booking theatre tickets.'

'Oh, you offer that as part of the service, do you?' I recalled having to stow bulky items of luggage beneath the reception desk at the Anthony in Leeds, and making dinner reservations for guests who didn't want to eat in the hotel restaurant, but this would all be new information to Jane, and I needed to react accordingly.

'Of course. Anything to make the guest feel like they're valued and important; like nothing is too much trouble for us. We have various leaflets detailing local attractions on that stand by the front door. You might want to familiarise yourself with them, so if you're asked where the nearest golf course is, or what time the pier attractions open, you'll know.' He paused. 'And, last but very definitely not least, you'll have to deal with any complaints or problems that might arise. Most of them you'll refer on to me, unless it's something you can deal with yourself, like someone needing more teabags in their room. If that happens, there's a box under the desk where we keep tea and coffee-making supplies that can be handed out, as well as shower caps, soap, sewing kits, and the like. All of those things are complimentary, of course.'

'Of course,' I echoed.

'Well, I think that's everything. The staff cloakroom is just round the corner, and there are lockers where you can leave your coat and bag. My office is just down the hall if you need me for anything. But unless it's an absolute emergency, call me on the phone. I'm on extension one. It's really important that you don't step away from the desk for any longer than you have to; it looks bad if a guest arrives and there's no one around to attend to them.' He made to walk away, before seeming to remember something. 'Oh, I almost forgot. I was going to show you the lift, wasn't I? Come with me.'

He led me across the lobby. The short walk gave me time to notice the slightly worn carpet and the dated, fussy pattern of the wallpaper. I felt as though I'd stepped back in time forty years: an impression that was reinforced when we reached the lift. It had heavy doors, designed to be opened and closed manually. The sight took me straight back to being a child of ten or eleven, and the summer holidays I'd spent in one or other of the family hotels, using all my strength to heave those doors shut before the lift would move.

'Wow, that looks like a real museum piece,' I commented, as Rhodri opened the outer door to show the second, ironwork door within. Again, this was of a concertina design, in an intricate lattice pattern.

'Don't worry; it's more reliable than the computers around here,' Rhodri assured me. 'And in a way, it'd be a shame to see it go. But head office seems to have decided that, for whatever reason, it's not economical to bring this place into the 21st century.'

'Do you have many dealings with head office?' I did my best to make the question sound casual.

'Not really. When I took this job, they said someone would visit on a regular basis, take a note of any concerns I had, but I haven't seen anyone in all the months I've been here. OK, so there was a change at the top of the company not long after I joined – Gus Anthony died suddenly, and his daughter, Claudia, took over – but she doesn't seem to have any more interest in this place than he ever did.'

'Maybe she's just busy?' I suggested, picking at a piece of fluff on the sleeve of my jacket and trying not to meet his gaze. I hoped Dean, still filming at a discreet distance, hadn't picked up on my sudden unease. I'd always told people I was happy to be criticised to my face, but this felt weird somehow, like eavesdropping on a conversation about myself. They always said no good ever came of doing that, and now I knew what they meant. 'I mean, it must be a lot for someone to take on, particularly when she's so young.'

Rhodri gave me a look as if to say, "How did you know that?"

I quickly covered myself by adding, 'I saw an article on Claudia Anthony in one of the glossy magazines when I was last at the hairdressers. It must have been some kind of omen because I found out I was going to be placed with this hotel for the documentary a couple of days later.'

He grunted, as though he didn't believe in omens. 'All I know is it would be nice to feel like my staff and I are valued for what we do, and that this hotel wasn't just viewed as some kind of pimple on the backside of the company ...' He seemed to remember his words were being caught on camera, and stopped himself going any further. 'But I have things to do, and you need to go back to the front desk. You'll be relieved for your lunch break at midday – you get half an hour– and then Tom, who's on evening duty at the moment, will be in just before you come off shift at four. Any other questions?'

'No, I think that's everything for now.'

'Great, well, if you need me, you know where I am. And Jane –' he smiled, and for the first time I really noticed the intense blue of his eyes, like the sky on a summer morning, '– despite the impression I might have given you, this isn't a bad place to work.'

41

With that, he hurried off in the direction of his office, leaving me to trudge back to the reception desk, wondering again what I'd let myself in for.

By the time Tom, who appeared to be no older than nineteen and looked like he was still growing into the fit of his baggy black suit, came to relieve me of my duties, I'd experienced the most boring day of my working life. I could count the number of guests I'd checked in and out on the fingers of one hand, and on every occasion, the reservation system had moved with the speed of an arthritic snail. Fortunately, everyone had accepted my apologies for the delay with good grace, though I had grown more embarrassed each time.

I'd taken a couple of calls from people wanting to book rooms, and rooted in the supply box beneath my desk to help out a woman who'd neglected to bring any toothpaste with her, but those had pretty much been the highlights of my day. The rest of the time I'd spent reading the leaflets Rhodri had pointed out to me, learning more about the places of interest along this stretch of the coastline, from the ruins of Castell Aberpentre, which had been destroyed in a battle with Edward I's forces in the late 13th century, to the nearby town of Criccieth, the Parliamentary constituency of David Lloyd George.

I wished Tom a pleasant evening and left the hotel. If I had to put up with another four weeks of this tedium, I didn't know how I'd survive. I only hoped Dean would be able to shoot enough interesting footage to stop the viewers of *Secret CEO* switching off in their droves when the programme was broadcast.

'Dean and I are off to the pub,' Bayo said as he packed away his recording equipment. 'You're welcome to join us

42

if you'd like.'

I shook my head. 'Thanks for the offer, but I really ought to go and get some food shopping done. And then I just want to fester in front of the TV in preparation for tomorrow's excitement. See you both in the morning.'

Back in the apartment, I sat on the sofa in my dressing gown, having enjoyed a long, scented bath. With a scratch-made chicken casserole cooking on the stove and a big glass of Merlot to hand, I started to feel a little brighter. Yes, today had been dull, but I'd already started to learn where improvements could be made to the hotel – assuming I decided not to recommend that we sell it, that was. Inspired, I went to dig in my handbag for the little video camera Dean had passed over to me that morning. I set it up on the table, set it recording, and spoke directly into the lens.

'Today's been an education for me. We've clearly been neglecting the Aberpentre Anthony, and to an extent, I can see why. But I'm ashamed that we're expecting the reservation software to run on computers that clearly aren't designed to handle it, and that guests are being kept waiting to check in as a result. That's just not acceptable, and I'm going to make sure we find the money in the budget to get those computers upgraded as soon as possible. The lift ... well, that was a real blast from the past. I didn't realise we had anything of that age still operating in any of our hotels, but replacing it is a big job, and at the moment this renovation strikes me as a case of taking baby steps – if we decide to go ahead with it, that is.'

I went to turn off the camera, then thought of something else. 'As for my first impressions of the staff –

to be honest, I haven't seen enough of any of them to judge, apart from Rhodri. His outburst when we were talking about the treatment he thinks the hotel is receiving was a little unprofessional, and if he came out with anything like that within earshot of the guests, I'd have to reprimand him. But the man has a straightforward quality about him, and an energy that I find intriguing. I'd hate to think he's getting so disenchanted with the company that he might be thinking of leaving after being with us for such a short time, because we really need people like him working for us. I don't know how I'll convince him to stay, but it's something I'm determined to do before this project is over ...'

This time, I did end the recording. Taking another sip of my wine, I sprawled back against the sofa cushions. When I closed my eyes, Rhodri's face swam into vision. I hadn't been lying to the camera; the man did intrigue me. And it wasn't simply because he had the look and attitude that inspired my rudest fantasies. Even though he was my boss – albeit on a temporary basis – I wanted to get to know him better.

Thinking about Rhodri, I felt heat start to build between my legs. I took another sip of my wine, then set the glass down carefully on the table. Slipping a hand under the opening of my dressing gown, I stroked the soft fullness of my breast. When I closed my eyes, I imagined that it was Rhodri touching me there, teasing my nipple into stiffness while his lips nuzzled my neck.

I moved my fingers lower, down over the slight curve of my belly to the apex of my thighs. Already, moisture had begun to pool there, and even that light touch had me squirming against the sofa cushions.

In my mind's eye, Rhodri stood before me. Taking my cue from the sassy heroine in the Jason Statham film I'd been watching the other night, I imagined that I was ordering him to take his clothes off for my pleasure. He pulled off his tie, and let it drop to the floor, then shrugged out of his jacket. The shirt came next, each button coming undone in methodical fashion. His chest, in my imagination at least, was broad, with a light dusting of dark hair across his pecs; hair that then descended in a thin line towards his crotch, still covered by his suit trousers.

Stroking myself while I pictured Rhodri stripping for me felt so good. Little thrills of pleasure shivered through my core as my fingers dabbled in my increasing wetness, but I needed more. In my bedroom drawer, I'd stashed my favourite vibrator, and now I went to find it. It wasn't anything fancy – just a thick length of neon pink silicon rubber that could vibrate at three different speeds – but right now it was just what I needed.

Having taken up my position on the sofa once more, I undid my robe and let my legs sprawl open. I resumed the fantasy where I'd left off, with Rhodri peeling out of his trousers, only now his striptease was accompanied by the low-pitched buzzing of the sex toy as I played it over myself.

'That's it,' I murmured into the silence of the room, 'take it off for me. Take it all off …'

My imaginary lover complied, easing down a pair of tight white briefs and freeing his cock. Already, it was almost fully erect, sticking out from his groin as if demanding to be touched. Rhodri turned in a slow circle, letting me get a look at his back view in the process. He had taut, round buttocks that I longed to sink my teeth into, and I lingered on that thought as I brushed the head of the vibrator over my clitoris.

'Such a beautiful boy,' I murmured to myself, 'and all mine ...'

The way I had intended the scenario to play out was to place him down on his knees once he was naked. I'd enjoyed similar fantasies before, always with some faceless lover who begged to satisfy my every desire. But tonight, I needed my fantasy Rhodri to be the boss in the bedroom, as well as the hotel. Though I hated to have anyone telling me what to do, the orders would sound right if they were issued from his lips. For once, I would give up all control, so that he could show me the pleasure that came from submitting.

Almost without being aware of it, I had placed the vibrator inside me, and now I pushed it fully home. The toy buzzed within me, its rhythmic vibrations spreading out and sweeping me away in a rush of sheer bliss. I felt myself convulsing around the soft silicon, and in the last lucid moment before my orgasm hit, I wished with all my heart that it was Rhodri buried so deeply inside me.

FOUR

The next couple of days crawled by. I barely saw Rhodri, who spent most of the time in his office. Though given the fantasy I'd had about him that was probably for the best. I had no desire for him to catch me blushing as I remembered how I'd pictured him stripping for me, and how I'd wanted to find myself down on my knees before him, waiting to obey his every instruction.

I'd half hoped to get a phone call or a chatty email from Kay, who'd wanted to be kept informed of how I was getting on. But she'd sent me a brief text to let me know her department was undergoing an unexpected audit, leaving her up to her eyes in work, and since then I'd heard nothing.

Dean seemed to have decided there was no point shooting endless hours of film of me doing nothing, which suited me just fine, though the lack of activity made its own statement about the state of affairs at the hotel. We'd known from the monthly figures we received at head office that occupancy rates here were on the low side, but they had never quite dipped to a level that alarmed us. And with the schools just about to break up for the May half-term holiday, things would get busier in the coming week – or so I hoped.

Still, when Rhodri appeared at the desk, I didn't know quite what to expect. I hastily pushed the Jodi Picoult paperback I'd been reading into my handbag and did my best to look alert.

'Hi, is everything OK?' I asked him.

'Jane, I need you to do me an enormous favour. One of the chambermaids rang in sick this morning, and I'd like you to fill in for her.'

'But ...' He couldn't ask this of me, surely? Nowhere was the task of cleaning rooms and making beds in my job description as receptionist. 'What about the front desk?'

'I'll cover that. It's not the first time I've had to do it. And you really would be getting me out of an enormous hole.'

He had a point. In all hotels, there's a limited period for the housekeeping team to perform its duties, and if one member of that team is missing, it means everyone else has to cover the shortfall, meaning less time spent on cleaning each room. Which is when standards can slip and guests find things to complain about.

I looked up and registered the sight of Dean training the camera in our direction. Presumably, he'd started filming when Rhodri arrived, hoping to capture something in the way of interaction between us. And now he was witnessing the first potential conflict between us.

I wanted to refuse – after all, I'd told Kay the one thing I was not prepared to do for this documentary was take on the role of a chambermaid – but I couldn't leave Rhodri in the lurch. More than that, I didn't want to come across as some kind of spoilt bitch who thought scrubbing toilets was beneath her.

'OK, just tell me what I have to do.'

'Fantastic, Jane, thank you so much. Come with me, and I'll introduce you to Wioletta, who's the head of housekeeping.'

Wioletta was short and stout, with a brisk, no nonsense manner. Her hair was pulled into a bun so tight it must surely induce headaches, and she regarded me with shrewd grey eyes, as if assessing my ability to push a housekeeping trolley. Once I'd swapped my skirt suit for the peach-coloured polyester overall that was the standard uniform for cleaning staff across the Anthony chain, she led me into the room where the cleaning supplies were kept.

'Now, Jane, Rhodri tells me you have never worked in as a chambermaid before.'

'No, but I have cleaned my own flat plenty of times.'

My attempt at humour didn't mollify her. 'This is nothing like cleaning a flat. You need to work fast, and you need to leave every surface so clean that you could eat your dinner from it. Now, the first thing you must do is stock your cart ...'

Under her watchful eye, I loaded the trolley with clean sheets, towels, and all the sundries for each room, from miniature bottles of shampoo and conditioner to coffee sachets and packs of Highland shortbread biscuits. I wasn't moving fast enough for her liking, and once or twice, she barked at me to hurry up. Once I'd added all the cleaning fluids I would need, along with cloths and brushes, we wheeled the trolley into the lift. It was a tight squeeze, with not enough room for Dean and Bayo to join us. They set about climbing the four flights of stairs to the top floor, and as the lift made its slow ascent, I reckoned they might reach it before we did.

I had so many questions to ask Wioletta about the room-cleaning process – the type of questions the inexperienced Jane would ask – but I knew Dean would want to capture that conversation on camera.

At last, the lift came to a halt, and I wrenched open the door, just in time to see the two men walking towards us. Dean, I couldn't help but notice, looked considerably more out of breath than Bayo.

I pushed the trolley along the corridor. When we reached the door of the first room, Wioletta told me to stop. 'Now,' she said. 'I talk you through cleaning this room. After that, you are on your own.'

'How long do we have for each room?'

'Twenty-five minutes. You work fast, you work hard, but most important of all, you work with a smile on your face.' It was the first time I'd seen her stony façade crack just a little, and I nodded to show I intended to follow her advice.

We knocked on the door. Getting no response, Wioletta unlocked the door with her master key card and we went inside. It didn't look too untidy in comparison to some I'd cleaned before, and I wondered whether Dean was disappointed not to capture my reaction on being faced with a level of room trashing to rival Led Zeppelin in their heyday.

We had a list to consult that told us whether each room was being prepared for new guests, in which case fresh bed linen would be needed, or whether we were cleaning it for someone who would be returning later that day. This particular room needed the full treatment.

As I stripped the sheets off the bed, I asked Wioletta,

'So, have you been working for the hotel long?'

'I have been here three years. I come to Wales because it is a very beautiful place, and there are always jobs here if you are prepared to turn up on time and work hard. Though one day I hope to return to Kraków … Now, you need to take the bedding, leave it in the corridor outside.'

Once I'd done that, I returned with fresh sheets and pillowcases from the trolley. Wioletta watched me like a hawk as I draped the bottom sheet over the mattress, tucking it in tightly.

'And what do you think about working for this company? How do they treat you?'

'I like it here. They pay well, compared to some of the other hotels in this town, and Mr Wynn-Jones, he is a good boss. But I have been here three years, like I say, and in that time I have four, maybe five different bosses. I do not think that is such a good way to run a business.'

I arranged the coverlet over the sheets, and placed a small, foil-wrapped chocolate on each pillow. Satisfied that I had made the bed to her exacting standards, she led me through to the bathroom.

'Here, you must work very fast,' she told me. 'You must check the towels – if they have been left in the bath, then it means the guest would like fresh ones. But as new guests are coming into this room, all the towels must be replaced as matter of course. And every surface must gleam by the time you have finished cleaning it.'

That seemed like a tall order in the time we had been allotted for each room, but memories of all the summers I had spent working as a chambermaid came back to me and I found myself needing less in the way of instruction. I made sure the little tray containing complimentary toiletries had the full range of supplies, and even remembered to wipe all the "hidden" places, like the strip of porcelain between the toilet seat and the cistern where dirt and stray hairs had a tendency to gather. It could have been my imagination, but I was sure I heard Wioletta give a soft grunt of approval as she watched me.

As I rinsed out the bathtub, I asked, 'What would make things better for you? Working here, I mean.'

I waited for her to reel off a list of improvements just as Rhodri had done when he'd been complaining about the computers, but she considered the question for a while and said, 'You know, I think mostly I am content. There is always more money that could be spent to make things better – that is true of life wherever you are – but if people walk into the rooms and are happy that they are clean and welcoming, then I am happy and I go home knowing I have done a good job.'

I rose from the side of the bath, about to compliment her on her attitude, when she snapped, 'The taps, Jane. You forget the taps, and they must gleam.'

As I sighed and got back into a kneeling position, I caught sight of Dean, reflected in the mirror I'd already polished until it shone. His camera was trained on me, capturing my reaction. I wanted to throw a duster to him and a scrubbing brush to Bayo, and order them to give me a hand so I could get this ordeal over quicker.

By the time I'd finished cleaning the nine rooms each member of the housekeeping team had been allotted, my back and knees ached and I could cheerfully have killed Rhodri for demanding this of me. However cute he might be, and however much he'd dressed this up as favour to him, I couldn't help imagining him sitting at the front desk right now, chuckling to himself at the thought of me up to my elbows in a toilet bowl.

At last, I dumped my J-cloth and bottle of surface cleaner on the trolley, rounded up the last of the towels and bedding that had been left in the corridor to be taken down to the laundry room, and wiped a few strands of my damp fringe out of my eyes. While Dean had pretty much given up on filming after the first couple of rooms, he made sure to train the camera on Wioletta and me as we wheeled the housekeeping cart into the lift. I must have looked like I'd run a marathon; my hair was lank, and there were distinct sweat patches on my overall. But at least I'd be able to freshen up in the staff cloakroom before returning to my duties in Reception.

'For your first time as housekeeper, you did very well, Jane,' Wioletta told me just before we pulled the lift doors shut. 'I would be happy to take you on as part of my team.'

Dean, did you hear that? That should definitely be part of the documentary, I wanted to call out, but already the lift was beginning its creaking descent. Still, I couldn't help but feel a glow of satisfaction at having received a compliment from my Polish taskmistress.

'Thanks, Wioletta, but Rhodri is going to need me back on the front desk.'

'Mr Wynn-Jones, he has something special in you. I hope he appreciates that.'

I wanted to ask her exactly what she meant by that, but when the lift stopped at the second floor, she got out.

'I must check that all the bedding has been collected and taken downstairs,' she told me. 'You must take this –' she gestured to the heap of used sheets and towels that we had piled on to the trolley, '– to the laundry room, then leave the cart where you found it. After that, you are done.'

'Of course.'

Wioletta heaved at the outer door, which stuck for a moment as she pulled it across.

'Always, this door is hard to close,' she muttered.

'Don't worry, I'll have a word with Rhodri about it,' I assured her. 'I'm sure he'll get someone to take a look at it. I'll bet it's nothing a good squirt of WD-40 can't sort out.'

As she'd asked, I delivered all the dirty laundry to be washed. When I went to return the trolley to housekeeping, Dean and Bayo were waiting for me.

'Hey, can we just do a quick piece to camera, babe?' Dean asked. 'I'd like to get your thoughts on the work you've been doing today while they're still fresh.'

Talking into his lens was the last thing I wanted to do, afraid I might reveal more of my thoughts than might be appropriate in the circumstances. 'I should really go and relieve Rhodri. He's bound to have things to do that are more important than manning the front desk.'

'Come on, it'll only take a minute …'

'OK.' I took a moment to compose myself. 'This morning has been some of the hardest work I've done in a long time, but despite what I said to Wioletta, it's not the first time I've cleaned guest rooms, and I've always been well aware of the pressure the housekeeping team in any hotel is under. Wioletta has a great work ethic, she takes pride in a job well done, and I think her attitude permeates through to the rest of her staff. I'd also like to hope that she feels sufficiently rewarded by us to not think about moving on to work in another hotel, and if that's not the case, then I'll look into what I can do about that on my return to head office.' I took a breath. 'And I was pleased to see that Rhodri was prepared to step in and take over the running of the front desk, though that's no more than I would expect of any of my managers in a similar situation.'

Seeing that I didn't intend to add anything else, Dean shut off the camera and set it down.

'That was great. But I think we need to have a chat …'

Something in the tone of his voice alarmed me. From what I knew, Dean had uploaded some of the footage he'd been shooting to his laptop, and had sent it over to the editors at Wild Card. Was there a problem with the content they'd seen? Were they thinking of calling a halt to filming? If so, it was just my luck if they only decided to make that decision after I'd spent most of the day changing bed linen and scrubbing bathtubs.

'I'm going to that sandwich shop round the corner; pick myself up a bit of lunch,' Bayo announced. 'Can I get either of you anything?'

'Yeah, I'd like a Coronation chicken baguette and a can of Diet Coke,' Dean said, reaching into his pocket for his wallet. He produced a £10 note and handed it to Bayo, then looked at me. 'And what are you having? It's on me.'

'Thanks,' I replied. Even though his generosity surprised me, I couldn't help wondering if it was a way of softening the blow to come. 'Can I have a tuna and avocado bap with Marie Rose sauce, please? Oh, and a bottle of fizzy water.'

'Sure. I'll be back in a few minutes.'

When Bayo had gone, Dean fixed me with an

apologetic look. 'There's something you need to know. I've been getting the feeling that you're mad at Rhodri for forcing you into helping the housekeeping team today. Well … it wasn't his idea. Not entirely.'

'What are you talking about?'

He squirmed under the force of my gaze. 'Hugo looked at the footage I sent over, and he … thought it was a bit dull. He'd expected there to be more in the way of tension between you and Rhodri.'

Oh, there's tension all right, I wanted to tell him. Just not the sort that's visible to the naked eye. 'Well, you can let him know I apologise for the fact we're not screaming and throwing things at each other, but I don't see how any of that equates to me having to work as a chambermaid.'

'Hugo knew it was the one job you really didn't want to do. He said you told him that when he first discussed your involvement in the programme. And he thought that if you were ordered to clean the bedrooms there might be –' he paused, '– "fireworks", I think is how he put it.'

The sneaky, manipulative son of a … I clapped him on the shoulder. 'Thanks for mentioning this to me, Dean; I really appreciate it.' I clapped him on the shoulder, about to turn and leave, then something occurred to me. 'But there's one thing I don't understand. How could Rhodri – or Hugo, for that matter – guarantee that one of the regular chambermaids was going to fall ill?'

'Oh, she's not really ill. Hugo said he was going to ask Rhodri to ring her last night and give her the day off. But I'd be grateful if you didn't let Rhodri know I told you about any of this.'

'Don't worry. Your secret's safe with me. I know that none of this is down to you. And I wish I wasn't stuck

56

doing this boring job in this boring little town, but I agreed to the project and I've got to see it out to the end. Now, I'd better go and get changed.' Tempted as I was to leave Rhodri stewing on the front desk just a little longer, I couldn't wait to get out of the frumpy overall, which by now was clinging to me. 'When Bayo gets back, if you could tell him to leave my lunch in Reception that would be fantastic.'

As I freshened up in the staff cloakroom, I considered Hugo Murray's devious attempt to inject some spice into his documentary. I'd heard stories that sometimes events were stage-managed to make things appear more dramatic, but I hadn't expected to be the victim of such underhand tactics myself. And why hadn't Rhodri said no to Hugo's plan? For all that there appeared to be no obvious friction between us, did he still resent my presence here? I couldn't ask him, not without dropping Dean in it. And like I'd told Dean, none of this was his fault, not really; he could only send over the footage he was able to shoot, and the fact nothing exciting happened in it wasn't down to him.

When I walked out into Reception, a paper bag and a bottle of water sat on the desk. 'Bayo dropped those off for you,' Rhodri said. 'Aren't you taking a lunch break, Jane? You're overdue one.'

'So are you,' I pointed out, 'and I'll probably pop out and get some fresh air shortly.' I unscrewed the bottle top and took a long swig, soothing my parched throat.

'Everything all right? Did you get on with Wioletta OK?'

'Put it this way, she was so impressed she's thinking of poaching me for the housekeeping staff.' I grinned. 'Don't worry; I'm not planning to take her up on the offer. But we did have a bit of a problem with the lift door on the second floor. She complained that it keeps sticking.'

'Yeah, one of the guests mentioned the same thing earlier on. I'll get someone from the maintenance crew to check it. Probably just needs oiling.' Rhodri vacated the space behind the desk. 'Thanks again for covering for Jade today.'

'No problem,' I assured him. 'Just let me know if you need me to do it again tomorrow.'

He shook his head. 'I don't think that'll be necessary. When I spoke to her, she said it was just one of those twenty-four hour things, you know?'

Yes, I believe they call them a day's holiday, I wanted to retort, but kept my mouth shut.

'Well, enjoy your lunch,' he said. 'I'm just off to get a sandwich of my own. If anyone calls, tell them I'll be back in ten minutes.'

He flashed me a little smile before sauntering out of the lobby. If he didn't want me here, he was doing a damn good job of disguising it. I needed to discover how he felt about me, and soon. If Hugo Murray was going to pull any more stunts like today's, I had to know whether I could count on Rhodri as an ally, or whether he too was prepared to watch me crash and burn in the pursuit of good television.

FIVE

Friday morning, and back in London, I would have been preparing for the monthly board meeting. As it was, I'd sent my apologies, along with an email telling the rest of the attendees that my time in Wales was already proving profitable, and I'd have plenty to discuss on my return. I'd checked the rest of my work emails, making sure nothing urgent had arisen that would need my attention. But everyone appeared to be coping perfectly fine in my absence. I didn't know whether to be relieved or disappointed.

For once, I didn't even have my friendly camera crew for company – Dean had gone down with an attack of food poisoning and was too ill to work. After yesterday's incident with the missing chambermaid, I'd wondered if this was just an excuse so he could take the day off and meet up with his boyfriend in Chester. However, Bayo had assured me that Dean was genuinely too sick to venture out of the apartment.

'He's a lousy patient. *The room's too bright, my pillows are too soft …*' he added, in a pitch-perfect imitation of Dean's voice. 'I'm going to make sure he's got plenty of Lucozade and a stack of comic books to keep him occupied, then I'm off to Criccieth for a round of golf.' Bayo should have sounded more apologetic than he did at leaving me alone, but I suspected that, like me, he'd already started going stir crazy within the confines of the hotel.

In an effort to keep myself occupied, I'd tidied up the leaflet stand, and sorted the magazines that were left on tables in the lobby for guests to read, making sure that the oldest and most dog-eared went in the recycling bin. Now, all I could do was sit and wait for the expected influx of weekend travellers to arrive.

I looked up as a girl entered the hotel and strutted across the lobby, her blonde curls bouncing on her shoulders. With her creamy complexion and wide, blue eyes, she reminded me irresistibly of a porcelain doll.

'Good morning, and welcome to the Anthony Hotel.' I smiled at her as I recited the standard greeting. 'Can I take your name?'

'Oh, I'm not staying here or anything. I'm here to see Rhodri.'

He hadn't mentioned that he was expecting a visitor, but as I'd learnt, he seemed to enjoy springing surprises on me to see how I'd cope. 'Do you have an appointment?'

Her laugh carried a note of condescension. 'You're new here, aren't you, love? I don't need an appointment. Tell him it's Angharad.'

'Just a moment, please.' I rang Rhodri's extension. He answered on the third ring. When he did, I said, 'Rhodri, I have an Angharad in Reception to see you.'

'Tell her I'm busy, Jane.' Before I could respond, he put the phone down on me.

I looked up at the visitor, smiling in an effort to

disguise my annoyance at Rhodri's uncalled-for rudeness. 'I'm afraid he's not available at the moment. Can I take a message?'

'Oh, he's always got time to see me. His office is along this way, isn't it?' She pointed down the hall. Before I could attempt to stop her, she was striding in that direction.

I redialled Rhodri. 'What now?' he snapped.

'Angharad is on her way to your office. I'm afraid I couldn't stop her.'

'Oh for fuck's sake ...' This time, he slammed the receiver down. I was glad Dean wasn't around to record this scene for posterity, because by now I could have punched a hole in the wall. Whatever the cause of the tension between Rhodri and this woman, there had been no need to drag me into it.

Ignoring the rule about leaving the front desk unattended, I ran after Angharad. Maybe I could head her off before she reached Rhodri's office. The sound of raised voices from behind the door let me know I was too late.

Though every instinct told me to walk away, I stood where I was, listening to the ensuing argument. 'What did I say about you coming to see me at work?' I heard Rhodri ask.

'Oh love, I know you didn't really mean that. And this was important. I wanted to give you some leaflets for the charity quiz night we're holding for the Aberpentre hospice at the wine bar, so you can pass them on to your guests.'

'You could have left those with Jane on Reception. You didn't need to bother me with this ... Look, Angharad, how many times do I have to tell you it's over between us?

And whatever you do, I'm not going to change my mind on that. Now, please, just go.'

'But you'll come to the quiz night?' she persisted.

I didn't wait to hear his answer; I suspected it wouldn't be polite. Needing to be back at Reception before Angharad left Rhodri's office, I dashed along the hall and took my seat once more.

She didn't say anything as she stalked out of the lobby, but the look she shot me could have blistered paint. I felt like I'd made an enemy without really understanding why.

Rhodri arrived at the front desk a couple of moments later. In his hand, he clutched a sheaf of leaflets. I half expected him to toss them into the bin, but instead he laid them down on the top of the desk. 'Would you mind adding those to the display stand?'

'Of course.' When he didn't immediately return to his desk, I said, 'Am I allowed to ask who that was?'

He sighed, and shifted uncomfortably from foot to foot. Clearly, he didn't want to talk about it, but I could be just as stubborn, and I wasn't going to let him walk away without some kind of explanation.

'OK. If you really must know, Angharad Williams is my ex-girlfriend. We went out for about a year, but it just didn't work out. There were no hard feelings when we split up, but recently she's been trying to get me back.'

'And you don't want that?'

'She's great, don't get me wrong, but she's a bit too much of a party girl for me. This job, it comes with a lot of responsibility; I can't be turning up at work with a hangover, or leaving early to go for a night on the town, and Angharad didn't seem to get that.'

'So now she's stalking you?'

'No, not stalking, exactly, but she does seem to find a lot of excuses to just bump into me, or to come down to the hotel for some reason or other.' He plucked at the corner of one of the leaflets. 'And I'm happy to help her promote this quiz night of hers. It's for a good cause, when all's said and done. But I'm doing my best to keep away from her, and that woman makes it so difficult for me. She couldn't spot a hint if it painted itself purple and walked along the sea front carrying a placard that said, "I AM A HINT". So what can you do?'

I laughed, despite myself. It did seem like Rhodri was doing his best to defuse a potentially difficult situation. But that didn't mean I was letting him off the hook for what had just happened, and he realised it.

'Thanks for understanding, Jane – and I'm sorry if I took my anger with Angharad out on you. That wasn't fair, and it wasn't professional.'

'Well, it's all forgotten now,' I assured him, just wanting to get back to work, rather than admit to myself how much his constant presence disconcerted me. Thoughts of him grovelling at my feet reminded me of the fantasies I'd woven about him, and caused a flush to heat my cheeks.

He took a couple of steps in the direction of his office, then paused and turned back to me. 'Look, I don't have to stay late tonight, for once, so why don't I buy you a drink after work, as a way of making it up to you? I mean, I've asked a lot of you the last couple of days, what with you having to help the housekeeping team yesterday. And we don't have to go anywhere near where Angharad works, even if it is the best wine bar in Aberpentre.'

'Well, I …' I searched frantically for an excuse, failed

to come up with one, and wondered quite why I was thinking of putting this man off. Just because he left me flustered and tongue-tied didn't mean I should turn down the opportunity of spending some time with him. Maybe he would turn out to be out to be so dull it would cure me of my secret cravings for him. 'Yes, that would be nice.'

'OK, why don't I meet you outside here at seven? We can decide where we're going from there.'

'That sounds like a plan.'

'Great, I'll see you then.

The rest of my shift dragged even more than usual. *It's just a drink with Rhodri*, I kept telling myself. *He realises he's been acting like a total arse towards you and he wants to apologise. Don't read anything more into it.* But I couldn't help myself. This was the closest I'd had to a date for the best part of a year, despite Kay's best efforts to fix me up with various eligible men of my acquaintance. Even though I'd sworn not to get involved with anyone, I couldn't help but feel a fluttering of nervous excitement at the thought of spending time with Rhodri away from the stifling atmosphere of the hotel.

Back at the apartment, I dithered for ages about what to wear. Nothing too dressy; nothing that looked like I was putting all the goods on display. Eventually, I went for a pretty yet casual look: skinny jeans and a strappy tunic top in a blue and white ditsy print. Along with a new wardrobe, I'd also had to acquire fresh make-up. The colours that suited me when I'd been blonde looked washed out against my dyed brown locks, so I'd replaced my usual raspberry lip stain with one in a deep plum tone. A striking collar necklace of silver and turquoise, a present from Kay on my last birthday, completed the outfit. A final check of my reflection in the mirror, and I was ready to go and meet Rhodri outside the hotel.

He certainly seemed to like my look, if the smile on his face as I approached was any indication. He swung himself down from the perimeter wall on which he'd been sitting, and walked towards me.

'Hey, Jane, I love your outfit.'

'Thanks. You don't look so bad yourself.' I'd never seen Rhodri in anything other than his neat work suit. Tonight, he had on a striped polo shirt and a pair of khaki shorts that revealed lean, lightly tanned calves. He swept a hand through his already tousled hair. Heat flooded through me in response to his casual gesture.

'So, are you hungry?'

Until he'd mentioned it, I hadn't even thought about food, but my stomach growled in response to his question. 'Starving.'

'Great, because I know the perfect place for dinner … Unless you're a vegetarian, that is. You're not, are you?' He sounded as though he should already know the answer to that question.

I shook my head.

'Wonderful. I mean, I don't have anything against people who don't eat meat, but …'

I'd never seen Rhodri look ruffled. It only made him appear cuter in my eyes.

'Rhodri, it's fine. I'm sure I'm going to enjoy this place.'

We fell into step as we walked along the promenade, heading in the direction of the pier. People were still down on the beach enjoying the evening sunshine, and out on the horizon, the outline of a slowly moving ship was visible. The bars and restaurants on this stretch of road looked busy, drinkers and diners spilling out to occupy the exterior tables. A pleasant, relaxed vibe hung like a heat haze over the sea front.

'It's a beautiful evening,' I said, wishing I'd brought my sunglasses with me.

'Yeah, and the forecast says the weather's set fair for the rest of the weekend, which is good. Means people might decide to come here on the spur of the moment, book an overnight stay to take advantage of the sunshine … Ah, here we are.'

We had turned down a side street, and now Rhodri came to a halt before a small, dimly lit restaurant. The sign over the door read Caffi Memphis. From the outside, it didn't look too promising, but I would trust Rhodri's judgement. As he guided me inside, he rested his hand on the small of my back for a moment. Just like the first time we'd shaken hands, I felt that same electricity. We had a connection, and this time I was sure he felt it too, but he said nothing.

The restaurant's interior was painted in a subtle shade of cream, with abstract paintings hanging on the wall and The Eagles' 'Take It to the Limit' playing over the sound system. A small, perky, blonde waitress greeted us. 'Welcome to Caffi Memphis. Do you have a reservation?'

'I'm afraid we don't,' Rhodri replied.

I glanced round. Of the dozen or so tables, almost all were occupied.

'That's not a problem,' the waitress said, 'I have a table for two in the corner. If you'd like to follow me …'

Once we were seated, she handed us each a menu and

left us to make our choices. I scanned the food on offer quickly, realising the clue had been in the restaurant's name. This place appeared to specialise in burgers and barbecued meat. Elvis himself would have approved.

'The pulled pork is amazing,' Rhodri, 'but everything they do is good. And they've been granted their drinks licence since the last time I was here. Before that, they had a "bring your own bottle" policy.'

'So they haven't been open all that long?'

'About nine months. Before that, this place was a dry cleaners.'

I wanted to ask whether he'd ever brought Angharad to Caffi Memphis, but I couldn't find a polite way of phrasing the question, and I wasn't entirely sure why it would matter so much if he had.

When the waitress returned, we ordered our drinks – a bottle of a locally brewed craft lager for Rhodri, and a glass of Merlot for me. Rhodri poured his lager into a glass, which he clinked against mine in a toast. 'Here's to things working out.' It seemed like a strange thing to say, but somehow appropriate under the circumstances.

We chatted about nothing of any real consequence until our food arrived. I'd followed Rhodri's suggestion and chosen the pulled pork bun, which came drizzled in a smoky barbecue sauce, with fries and house-made coleslaw on the side. Rhodri had gone for a burger topped with cheese, bacon, and spicy chipotle mayonnaise.

At the first bite of my pork, so tender it almost dissolved on my tongue, I let out a whimper of pure appreciation.

'Good?' Rhodri asked with a grin.

With a mouth full of food, all I could do was nod, sure

my expression gave away how much I was enjoying it.

At last, I set my cutlery down on a plate on which only a couple of stray fries and a smear of barbecue sauce remained.

'If bringing me here was your way of apologising for the last couple of days, then that apology is very much accepted.'

Rhodri licked mayonnaise from his fingers, an act that almost had me whimpering as loudly as the pork had done. 'Why do I get the feeling you're still a little bit mad at me?'

'Not mad,' I assured him, 'not at all. I just haven't been entirely sure where I stand with you. After all, you didn't give the impression you wanted me around, and then you shunted me off to work for housekeeping at the first opportunity ...' Even though I knew that had been Hugo Murray's doing, I couldn't admit it to Rhodri. And a mean-spirited little part of me was enjoying watching him squirm in response to my accusation.

'OK, so maybe we got off the wrong foot,' he said at length, 'but you have to appreciate I wasn't looking forward to having someone brought in to work in the hotel just for the purposes of some reality show.'

His thoughts were an uncanny echo of my own when the proposal had first been put to me, but I still felt compelled to point out, 'You could always have said no.'

'And how would that have gone down with senior management? If I come across as obstructive and resistant to new proposals, what are my chances of advancing in the company?'

'So you're thinking of promotion?' I tried to keep the surprise out of my voice. I'd become used to the managers we employed in Aberpentre looking for a swift exit from the company, rather than seeking to rise within its ranks.

'Not right now, but at some point. I mean, Aberpentre's where I was born, and I'm proud of the fact I'm running the best-known hotel in town and I'm not even thirty yet. But that doesn't mean I want to stay here for the rest of my life.' He sipped thoughtfully at his pint. 'And what about you, Jane? What are you hoping to get out of this documentary?'

'To be honest, I hadn't really thought about it,' I said, all too aware the documentary Rhodri believed he was taking part in wasn't the one that was actually being made. 'Maybe I'm hoping it will put me in the shop window; let people know I'm available for work. When you've been out of a job as long as I have, you'll pretty much consider anything that places you in front of a potential employer.'

'Well, I suppose it would make your CV stand out from the rest.'

'And I'm not the only one being filmed for this programme.' I recalled the fake backstory I'd been given by the team at Wild Card. 'There's a girl who left the Swansea Uni last summer with a degree in law. She hasn't been able to get a job in the legal profession, and so she's been found a placement at a care home in the Rhondda. And the other woman they're following worked on the local paper in Cardiff till she was made redundant, and they've got her working in a management position in a fast food restaurant. The idea is to show that in the current labour market you have to be flexible, look at all your options. Think about retraining, learning a new set of skills …'

A commotion at a neighbouring table distracted me. I

looked round to see a group of girls whooping and cheering as one of their number was presented with a wedge of chocolate fudge cake. A couple of fizzing sparklers and a candle had been pressed into the icing. The waiter struck up the first line of 'Happy Birthday', and the girls' friends joined in, to her obvious embarrassment.

'Hey, it's Friday evening,' I reminded Rhodri. 'Do you really want to be talking about work? Especially when that cake looks so delicious.'

'Yeah, I guess you're right.' He beckoned to our waitress. 'Could we have the dessert menu, please?'

'Oh, I don't think we need that,' I cut in. 'A piece of the chocolate fudge cake, please, and two forks.' Only when the waitress disappeared did I realise my actions might have come across as just a little bit domineering. 'I'm sorry, that was rude of me. Did you want something else?'

'No, cake's always a good choice. I'm just not used to a woman who's so decisive. When I went anywhere with Angharad, she'd always dither for ages about what she wanted, or she'd say she just wanted a salad or something, and then she'd start eating all the chips off my plate ...' His voice trailed off. 'I'm sorry; I'm sure you don't want to hear about Angharad.'

'Oh, it's all right. We're all guilty of going on about our exes,' I assured him, remembering all the times Kay had accused me of doing just that. What would she say, I wondered, if she could see me now, enjoying dinner with my temporary boss?

'Well, I promise I'll try not to do it again.'

'Hey, she was obviously a big part of your life. The things you did together are bound to come up in conversation, particularly if you're talking to someone who knows both of you. You can't just pretend none of that happened. It's different if you can make a clean break from someone; it makes it easier to start all over again.'

It had to be obvious I spoke from experience. From the way Rhodri looked at me, he had to be wondering whether that could be another reason I was so keen to move to a new town in the search for work.

'You know, Jane, I'm starting to realise you're not the person I thought you were.'

My stomach clenched with anxiety, but I told myself there was no way he could have worked out my real identity. His next words bore that out.

'When I first met you, I thought you were one of these pushy wannabes who'll do anything to get on TV. But you're nothing like that. You're smart, you're funny, you're not afraid of hard work, and you talk a lot of sense …'

Rhodri paused as the waitress placed a plate containing a generous slice of fudge cake on the table between us. He picked up his dessert fork and urged me to do the same. 'Go on, dig in.'

We descended on the cake like a pair of locusts, devouring it with quick, greedy bites, then Rhodri called for the bill. I brought my purse out of my handbag, offering to pay my share, but he waved the suggestion away. 'Tonight is on me.'

It was just as well. When I glanced in my purse, I saw only a few pound coins and some change. With my credit card bearing my real name, I couldn't use that and run the risk of Rhodri noticing the discrepancy.

'Well, let me leave a tip, at least.' I tossed a handful of coins into the saucer that contained the bill, snatched up

71

one of the peppermints already sitting there, and popped it into my mouth.

The night air held a definite chill as we stepped outside. Glad I'd thought to bring a jacket, I slipped it on. Rhodri still wore only his short-sleeved shirt, but he didn't seem to feel the cold.

We walked in companionable silence. The volume of the music coming from the sea front bars had kicked up a few notches. Maybe a few years ago, I would have been suggesting that the night was still young, and we could hit one of those bars for a few drinks and some dancing. But I had another early start tomorrow. Like Rhodri, I had responsibilities, and I needed to take them seriously.

We'd passed the Anthony, and almost before I'd realised it, we were standing on the pavement in front of the Bay Vista apartments.

'Well, this is me,' I said. 'Thanks for walking me home, and for a lovely meal. I can't remember when I last had such a good time.'

'Yeah, it's been fun. Maybe we could do it again.'

'We'll have to. I owe you dinner, don't I?'

He stepped a pace closer, and I looked up at him, silhouetted in the subdued orange glow of a streetlamp. Even though I wore heels, he still had a good few inches on me. Tension hung in the air between us.

I parted my lips a fraction, though whatever I'd intended to say was swallowed up as Rhodri swooped down to claim my mouth with a kiss.

His lips were soft against mine, and I brought my hands up to twine round the back of his neck as I raised myself up on my toes. There was a moment's awkwardness as I manoeuvred so my unfamiliar glasses weren't poking against my flesh, or his, and then I settled into the kiss. It was deep, intense; my body seeming to melt against his. Rhodri's tongue explored the contours of my mouth and I moaned, the sound swallowed up by the night.

He grabbed my bum cheeks in both hands and pulled me tight to him, breaking the passionate lip-lock so he could trail soft kisses over my neck and down to the hollow of my throat. With our bodies pressed together, I was all too aware of his cock, thick and solid, pushing at me. Even the layers of clothing between us failed to disguise its heat and urgency. He wanted me, just as much as I wanted him.

Heat burned between my legs. We gazed into each other's eyes. Maybe things were moving too fast here, but I didn't care. I was more than ready to take this further.

I was about to suggest that we go up to my apartment, where we could have a little privacy, when Rhodri's phone rang. *Ignore it, please,* I urged him silently. But already he was digging into his shorts pocket to retrieve it.

'Shit,' he murmured, looking at the caller display. 'I'm really sorry, Jane, but I've got to take this. It's Tom. He knows not to ring unless it's really urgent.'

I huddled into my jacket as Rhodri spoke urgently into the phone, the heat we'd generated with our passionate kisses already cooling.

'Yeah, sure ... I understand. Just make sure everyone meets at the evacuation point in the car park and I'll be there as soon as I can. You're lucky; I'm only a couple of minutes away.'

'What is it?' I asked, noticing the strain on Rhodri's face as he tucked his phone back in his pocket.

'The fire alarm's gone off. It could be nothing, but I've

got to go over there, make sure everything's OK. If nothing else, I'll have to check the system's been reset. Tom's making sure all the guests evacuate their rooms promptly.'

'Is there anything I can do?'

He shook his head. 'Thanks, Jane, but I've got this sorted.' He pressed another kiss to my mouth, one that had me wishing I could somehow persuade him to let Tom sort the situation out. But I knew nothing I could do would sway him. 'Thanks for a fantastic evening. We'll do it again, I promise.'

And with that, he was gone, haring down the street to the Anthony, and whatever problems might await him there. I watched till he disappeared from sight, then turned to go inside, tracing a finger along my lips as if I could still feel the softness of Rhodri's kiss there.

SIX

Getting out of bed the next morning took a real effort. On Saturdays, I'd become used to allowing myself the luxury of a lie-in till around eight o'clock before hitting the gym. Then I'd meet Kay or one of my other girlfriends for lunch and a little retail therapy in the shops of Knightsbridge or South Molton Street. I'd decided when Dad had first appointed me to the board of Anthony Hotels that my weekends would be work-free zones, and I'd done my best to stick to that principle ever since. Burning yourself out needlessly is no way to run a company, and I couldn't help wondering if my father might have added a few more years to his life if he'd known how to relax.

Today, however, I had to be on front desk duty at eight. Tempted as I was to roll over and have another half-hour in bed, I pulled on my jogging gear, and set off on my usual morning circuit.

As I ran, my thoughts drifted back to the night before, and dinner with Rhodri. I'd seen the fun-loving side of him he kept hidden away at work, but I'd also become aware of how seriously he took his responsibilities as hotel manager. We'd made a connection – or, rather, he'd made one with Jane. Would he have been so relaxed, so happy to share his dreams of progressing within the company, if he'd known he was really talking to his boss?

And the kiss ... I recalled the feel of his lips against mine, the heavy, insistent pressure of his erection against my stomach. If I'd asked him up to my apartment, I had no doubts things would have gone further. Maybe I wouldn't have woken up alone this morning.

Perhaps it was just as well that Rhodri had been called away just when things were growing intense. I didn't fall into bed with men at the first opportunity; it had never been in my nature. I liked to get to know them first. But then I'd thought I known Gavin well enough to let him into my bed, and my heart, and all the time I'd been unaware of his real motives for wanting to marry me.

Why was I even thinking about getting involved with Rhodri anyway? In a little over three weeks, filming would be over, and I'd be on my way back to London. The production team had told me that there'd be a big reveal at the end of the show, when all the people I'd been working with would learn my real identity. How awkward would meeting Rhodri under those circumstances be, if we'd slept together? Maybe it would be better all round if I kept our relationship on a light, friendly footing, but made it clear there were lines I wasn't prepared to cross.

I was still mulling the problem over when Rhodri walked into Reception shortly before lunchtime. All my resolve to keep a distance from him melted in the face of his affectionate smile.

'Hey, Jane, how's it going?'

'Fine. The people in Room 9 have complained their TV isn't working properly, and Owen from maintenance has

76

just gone up to see if he can find out what's wrong with it.'

'Well, it looks like you've got everything under control. Oh, and about last night ...'

'What about it?' I kept my tone light, waiting for him to tell me it had been a mistake, and that it wouldn't happen again.

'I had a great time with you, and I'm sorry I had to dash off like that.'

'So what happened about the fire alarm?' I asked, recalling the cause of his abrupt departure.

'Turned out it was one of the guests having a crafty cigarette in bed and setting the smoke alarm off. Why people do that when we have a strict no-smoking policy in all the bedrooms I'll never know. Still, no harm done – apart from the waste of the fire brigade's time, of course.'

'Does this sort of thing happen often?'

'Thankfully, no. This is only the second time the alarm's gone off while I've been the manager, outside of a routine drill. The last time, we had a rugby team from the valleys staying with us. A couple of them got back from a late-night bender and their prop forward decided to set the alarm off at one in the morning as a prank. They're banned from the hotel now, you won't be at all surprised to hear.'

'Well, at least you know Tom can cope with the evacuation process.' More importantly, so did I. It was another plus point on the list I was making when it came to the ability of Rhodri and his staff to run a successful hotel.

'Yeah, it'll be a shame when he goes.'

'Tom's leaving?' My heart sank. What was it about this place and staff retention?

'Not until September. He was telling me last night that

he's got a place on a college course in Cardiff. Business management. He said when he went for the interview the panel was very impressed he was working in for the Anthony chain. Apparently, the name carries a lot of weight, which hopefully should bode well for you when you start looking for jobs.'

'Assuming I decide to go into the hotel industry,' I said lightly. 'There's still time for you to put me off the idea for life, Mr Wynn-Jones.'

'And why would I do that?' He grinned, responding to my teasing. 'Actually, talking about Tom reminds me why I needed to speak to you. I'd like you to take the night shift for a week, starting Monday, so you can get a feel of what things would be like if you were with us on a full-time basis.'

'Of course,' I replied, wondering whether this was another of Hugo Murray's little schemes. 'Though to be honest, I've never worked nights. I pulled the odd all-nighter when I had to meet a deadline for filing accounts, but that's different.'

By now, it no longer surprised me how easily I adjusted to Jane's mind-set when the conversation required it. I had no problems imagining the person I might have become if I hadn't had the good fortune to be the heir to a thriving business.

'Yeah, I think we've all been there. Paperwork – it's the bane of my life. Anyway, our receptionists normally work on a rotating shift cycle – a month on mornings, a month on evenings, and then a month on nights. But this isn't a regular change to that pattern. I just need you to fill in for Morwenna. She's taking the week off as her kids are off school.'

At least that sounded like a genuine excuse, not something that might have been cooked up in the Wild Card office on the spur of the moment. 'It must be difficult for her, working shifts when she has children,' I commented.

'Not as much as you'd think. Her husband's some kind of IT professional. He works mostly from home, and that means there's always someone around to pick the kids up and drop them off from school.'

I nodded. It wasn't necessarily the kind of arrangement I'd want if I were married. But if it suited her and her husband, it couldn't be a bad thing. 'OK, so who'll be taking the shift I should be doing, if Morwenna's away and Tom's on mornings?'

'We have an agency we use for holiday cover. The people they send to us are always reliable …' He thought for a moment. 'Hey, that's an option you might want to consider. Once you've done your stint in the Anthony, you could get yourself on the books of some agencies. People are always looking for staff to cover a week here and there. I'd be happy to give you a reference if you need one.'

Rhodri's thoughtfulness surprised me, and I beamed at him. 'That's a great idea. I hadn't thought about temporary work.'

'Hey, I've been lucky; I've never been out of work for any length of time. But I've got mates who have, and it must be soul-destroying if you haven't got anything to get up for in the mornings. If I can do anything to help you get that job you've been looking for …'

'Thanks very much. And I won't say I'm exactly looking forward to working the night shift, but I suppose it's another point in my favour when it comes to impressing future employers.'

'That's the attitude, Jane.' And Rhodri strolled back to the office, leaving me with the impression of a man who'd crossed yet another item off his "to do" list.

Sunday was my day off, and I spent a good proportion of it sitting in the nearest laundrette, reading a book while my washing whirled in the machine. Then I tidied up the apartment. The task was no less boring than when I'd been cleaning rooms in the hotel, though at least I didn't have Wioletta at my elbow while I scrubbed the bath, urging me to make sure that everything gleamed.

I wasn't scheduled to start my shift till midnight the following day, and I pottered round for most of the afternoon, making a big pot of vegetable soup so I'd have something to take to work in a Thermos. Kay would have laughed at the concept of me owning something as mundane as a vacuum flask, but I knew there'd be almost nowhere open to grab a snack when I took my mid-shift break at four in the morning.

I wondered how the boys in Apartment 4 had been spending their day. Dean hadn't been thrilled to learn my shift had been changed. 'It's all right for you,' he'd grumbled to Bayo. 'You sit up half the night playing *FIFA 14*; you're practically nocturnal as it is. I need my beauty sleep ...'

'You'll get it, mate,' Bayo had pointed out. 'All you need to do is grab some shut-eye during the day. And it's not like we'll need to be there every night. It'd be the perfect time for you to take a couple of days off, go over and see Maurice in Chester like you wanted to.' He'd turned to me. 'And you won't need us there all the time; you can take your video camera in, and sit and record yourself if anything exciting happens. All alone in that spooky old hotel, night after night … It'll be just like *The Shining*.'

'Yeah, and you're the one I'll be chasing round the corridors with an axe, if you don't shut up,' I'd retorted good-naturedly. I knew I couldn't expect the boys to hang round the hotel on the off chance that something might happen – after all, they'd had little enough to film during the day – but their company would have been welcome during the long, boring shifts.

'I suppose you're right.' Dean's grumpy mood had brightened. 'It's only for a week, and then we're back to normal – or whatever passes for normal around here.'

I hadn't been expecting Rhodri still to be in the hotel when I arrived on Monday evening, but he was in Reception, chatting to Dean and Bayo. Catching the tail end of the conversation, I realised the three of them were discussing Cardiff City's prospects in some football play-off game, and tuned out. Football didn't hold any interest for me. Gavin had taken me along to watch his beloved Fulham a couple of times in the early days of our relationship, but I'd never warmed to the sport.

'Not got a home to go to, Rhodri?' I quipped, as I went to stash my handbag in one of the lockers just off the Reception area.

He followed me through so he could talk to me. I was aware of Dean filming from a discreet distance as I checked my lipstick in the little mirror on the back of the locker door. 'I realised I need to walk you through the

81

security checks the night duty receptionist is expected to make, particularly after the fire alarm went off the other night. As manager, I need to have full confidence that all my staff would be able to cope in the event of an emergency.'

'Well, I already know that whoever's on Reception has to supervise the evacuation procedure, as well as calling you to let you know what's happening. That's what Tom did on Friday, isn't it?'

'Of course, but they also have to make sure nothing's obstructing the fire doors on any of the floors, and check that none of the extinguishers are missing.'

'Who on earth would want to take one of those?' I asked, then remembered his story about the rugby team and the chaos they'd caused. I could quite easily see them setting off a fire extinguisher or two for a laugh. Good hotel management, Dad had reminded me on so many occasions, involved not only dealing with any issues that arose, but also anticipating those that might and having a strategy to cope with them. As luck would have it, we'd never suffered a serious fire on any of our properties, and all our staff needed to take whatever steps were necessary to ensure that remained the case.

'We'll start on the top floor and work our way down,' Rhodri told me, leading me in the direction of the lift. 'Are you OK with that?' he asked Dean.

'Sure. I've been meaning to take more exercise for a while, and climbing all those stairs is as good a way to do it as any, I suppose,' Dean grumped. 'We'll see you up there.'

As we waited for the lift, Rhodri said, 'If you'd been working the evening shift, I'd have shown you how to do these checks then. If you need to make any kind of inspection, it's always good to do it when it's quiet upstairs, and at that time of night, most people are having dinner in the restaurant, or they've gone out to eat if they're on a bed and breakfast only deal.'

'Do you get many people choosing to do that?' Most of the people I'd checked in were staying half board, with their breakfast and evening meals included.

'It's got more popular recently, particularly as we've been offering reduced-price B&B stays via a couple of those websites that offer daily voucher deals.'

I knew all about those deals; I'd been instrumental in setting the first one up, even though Dad had resisted the idea. He thought that offering cut-price deals weakened our brand, but I'd seen it differently. For a hotel like this, where rooms all too often went empty, anything that boosted occupancy rates could only help, even if it might mean making a small loss on each stay.

'Oh, I use those sites,' I said, knowing someone like Jane would always be looking for ways to save cash. 'I treated myself to one of those fish pedicures at a place in Caernarfon.' This was only half a lie; I'd tried the procedure, but it had been a birthday treat from Kay, as part of a spa day at an upmarket salon in Kensington.

'Fish pedicure?' Rhodri looked at me, his eyebrow raised.

'Yes. You put your feet in a tank full of these little fish, and they nibble all the hard skin away.' I chuckled in response to the face he pulled. 'Yeah, it's just as weird as it sounds. And you never realise quite how ticklish your feet are until you've got a shoal of tiddlers snacking on them.'

The lift arrived. We got in, and Rhodri pressed the

button for the top floor. For two and a half floors, we ascended smoothly, then there was the sound of metal grinding against metal, and the car juddered to a halt.

'What the ...?' Rhodri jabbed at buttons on the panel by the door, but nothing happened. He waited a moment, then tried again, with the same result. 'Shit! It looks like we're stuck.' He sighed. 'And I got the maintenance crew to look this thing over today as well.'

'So what do we do now?'

Rhodri pressed another button, which bore the image of a bell. 'That's the alarm. It should let the company that monitors the lift know there's a problem. Unfortunately, this thing's so old, it doesn't have any form of communication system built into it, so I can't speak to them directly.'

'Hopefully Bayo and Dean will realise something's wrong when the lift doesn't arrive at the top floor. They might be able to do something.'

'True, but even if they open the outside door, we're halfway between floors. I don't think we'd be able to climb out, and I don't want to risk trying it.'

'So we've just got to wait until someone arrives to get us out? How long is that going to take?' I'd never suffered from claustrophobia, but something about being trapped in this little metal box caused nausea to churn in my belly. Even Rhodri's solid presence by my side didn't seem to help. I shivered, and wiped suddenly clammy palms on my skirt.

'Hey, Jane, it's going to be OK.' He put an arm around me and gave me a reassuring hug. Though his intention was clearly to try and soothe me, he only succeeded in making things worse. I hadn't cried since the day of Dad's funeral, and now all the tears I'd been bottling up came flooding out.

'But it's the middle of the night,' I babbled into his shoulder, no longer sure what was really upsetting me. 'Who's going to come now?'

'They have people on call twenty-four hours a day. If anything, they'll be here quicker than they otherwise might. No traffic on the roads, no other idiots making demands on their attention by deciding to use an unreliable, thousand-year-old lift at midnight ...'

He held me tighter as my sobs turned into giggles at his exaggerated response to our predicament. At last, I pulled away from him and removed my glasses so I could wipe at my eyes. Rhodri dug into his pocket and found a handkerchief, which he passed to me.

'There you go, Jane. I just hate to see a woman cry.'

'I'm sorry.' I clutched the hankie in my fist. 'I don't know what came over me. Maybe I've watched too many horror films where people get trapped in lifts and terrible things happen to them.'

'So would now be the right time to tell you that we have a ghost here?'

'Really?' I thought I'd heard all the stories about the hotel, but this was news to me.

He shook his head. 'No. But it'd be pretty cool if there was. Just imagine if the spirit of some old hotel porter walked the landings, shining his torch as he went. Or if the place was haunted by an Edwardian lady who threw herself from one of the balconies because she'd been jilted by the man she was about to marry ...' His voice had dropped to a whisper, and as I spoke, something touched the back of my neck.

I shrieked and jumped backwards. Then realised what I had felt were Rhodri's fingers, moving in a spidery trail over my skin.

'That wasn't funny,' I snapped, as Rhodri fought to stifle his laughter. 'You have a morbid imagination, you know that?'

'So you don't want to swap ghost stories, then? Never mind, I'm sure we can find some other way of passing the time …'

In the dim glow of the emergency lighting, Rhodri's eyes were dark with desire. An air of anticipation hung between us, just as it had last night, in the moment before he kissed me. What had I told myself about not getting involved with him? It would be too complicated, too fraught with danger. Yet, as he pulled me into his arms again, I made no effort to resist.

Our lips were inches apart. I closed my eyes in anticipation.

The mood was broken as a repeated banging sound came from somewhere just above us. 'Hey!' called a deep voice that I recognised as Bayo's. 'Rhodri! Jane! Can you hear me in there?'

Were Rhodri and I destined to be interrupted every time it looked like we might share a romantic moment?

Rhodri didn't let go of me. He just raised his head and yelled, 'Yeah, you're coming through loud and clear. Where are you?'

'We're at the lift entrance on the third floor. We've pulled the door open and we can see the top of the car, but you're too far down for us to try and get to you.'

A vision swam into my mind of the lanky Bayo shinning down the lift cables to reach us, while Dean

86

filmed the heroic rescue. It would be just the kind of drama *Secret CEO* thrived on.

'Well, I've activated the alarm,' Rhodri told him, 'and someone from the lift company should be on their way over. The best thing you can do is go down to Reception and wait for them to arrive ... Oh, and there are some "Out of Order" signs in the room where we keep all the housekeeping supplies and stuff. If someone could hang one of those of each of the lift doors, it'll stop anyone trying to use them.'

'Sure, no problem. But you two are all right in there?'

'Jane and I are fine, honestly, mate. Don't worry about us.'

The silence stretched out as we waited for Bayo's reply, but when none came, I assumed that he and Dean had done as Rhodri suggested and gone downstairs.

'So,' Rhodri said, gazing down at me, 'no more panic, no more interruptions ...'

I stopped his words with a kiss, pressing my mouth hard against his. If the force of my actions surprised him, his only response was a slight widening of his eyes.

Rhodri tugged my jacket off, and it fell to the floor. We staggered back a couple of paces, till his back was up against the wall of the lift. My hands tangled in his dark hair as his lips nuzzled at my ear. I wanted him, never mind the consequences. Adrenaline coursed through my veins, stoked by fear and need, and I clung to Rhodri as though I was drowning and he was my life preserver.

'I dreamed about this last night,' he murmured against my ear. 'Kissing you, tasting you, having you warm and naked in my arms ...'

I moaned in answer. The images his words created

caused my inner muscles to flutter. I wanted to be naked for Rhodri, to give him everything he desired. To see the wild, unfocused look in his eyes as my body engulfed him.

He hoisted me up, his hands gripping my bottom securely, and I wrapped my legs around the small of his back. In this position, only the thin barrier of our clothing kept our most intimate places apart.

Rhodri kissed my neck, nuzzling the place just below my ear where my pulse beat fiercely. I threw back my head, giving him greater access as his mouth moved lower.

Made wanton by passion, I thumbed one of my own nipples through my blouse. It stiffened to a peak as I strummed it. I wanted Rhodri's lips on that tight bud, sucking it till it ached.

He guided me back down to my feet and spun us round, so that now I felt the chill of metal against my back. It did nothing to cool my overheating desire.

Stepping back from me for a moment, he shrugged off his jacket, then resumed kissing me. I plucked at the buttons on his shirt, undoing them with fingers made clumsy by my urgency to have him bared to me. Rhodri mimicked my actions, pulling my blouse wide open so he could kiss the curves of my breasts where they peeped above the ivory bra cups. He moved lower, till he mouthed my nipple through the cotton.

'More,' I begged, when he pulled his lips away, leaving wet fabric clinging to the swollen buds.

'All in good time.' He went to unclasp the front catch of my bra. I put my hand over his; stilling his actions as a thought struck me. 'Is there CCTV in this lift?'

His lips curved in a grin. 'I already told you; this thing is a thousand years old. CCTV wasn't invented when it was built, and we've never had the money to get it installed in here. Don't worry. No one's going to find out what we're doing. Unless you want them to, of course?'

I shook my head. This would be our dirty little secret; the moment when I broke all my self-imposed rules and let this gorgeous man possess me.

Now he popped the bra open, taking one of my breasts in his hand, weighing the fullness of it.

'I need you to fuck me,' I murmured, hardly able to believe the words came from my own lips. I'd never made such a direct request to anyone before; this wasn't like me at all. But then I wasn't myself any longer – at least, not as far as Rhodri was concerned. To him, I was Jane. And maybe Jane was the part of me who would let a man she barely knew strip her in a lift; who would beg for sex, and who would not be ashamed to make him aware just how much she needed him.

To back up my words, I yanked at his belt. Once that was undone, I turned my attention to his trousers, opening the fly so I could reach in and grasp his cock through his underwear. His breath hissed through his teeth, and I smiled at the reaction I'd coaxed from him. Usually, I was the passive one, letting things happen at my lover's pace, but being confined with Rhodri had made me reckless.

'Oh yes …' Rhodri's voice cracked around the words as I continued to stroke him, relishing the weight and heat of him even through the clinging jersey.

'Does that feel good?' I eased the front of his shorts down, so his length sprang free, hard and pulsing in my hand.

'Mm-hm. But before things go too far, I need to take care of something …'

He broke away from me, fished his wallet from his back pocket, and brought out a small foil packet from inside it. Until that moment, I hadn't even thought about protection. Rhodri had been a step ahead of me.

'Let me,' I said, taking the condom package from him and ripping it open. Rolling the thin latex down his shaft gave me another chance to hold and admire him.

We had to move fast. For all I knew, the man from the maintenance company had already arrived, and was working to restore power to the lift.

Rhodri had picked up on my urgency. He tugged at my tights and underwear, pulling them down in one swift movement. I felt the nylon snag and tear in his haste to undress me. Next time, I'll wear hold-ups, I thought, then reminded myself sharply to think of this as nothing but a one-off.

He pushed a hand between my legs, smiling to himself as his fingers made contact with the wetness. 'God, you're soaking, Jane. So ready for me.'

With that, he lifted me just as he had done before, guiding me into position so that when gravity pulled my body down, I slid onto his upstanding cock. My eyes widened as I registered the thickness of him; it had been longer than I could remember since I'd tried to take anyone – or anything – of his size.

'I'm not hurting you, am I?' Concern was evident in his tone, and I knew that if I said yes, he'd put a stop to this right now.

'No, I'm fine. It – it's just been a while.'

'OK, but if it gets too much, just let me know.'

He thrust up into me, slowly at first, then picked up the pace. Soon, every stroke slammed me against the wall of the lift, driving the breath from me. I clung on to him, my nails leaving white half-moons in the flesh of his shoulders as we panted and shuddered together. Rhodri's face was buried in the exposed flesh of my breasts, and he licked and nuzzled my nipples.

Delicious sensations rippled through my core. I dropped a hand down to where our bodies were joined, and rubbed my clit, knowing I didn't have the luxury of stringing this out, however much I wanted to. Just at the moment when my inner muscles clamped down hard on Rhodri's length and my pleasure crested, the lift creaked and lurched, threatening to knock him from his feet.

He gave one last, tormented groan, and I knew he too had reached his peak. We pulled apart from each other and I sank down the wall, feeling the blouse I still half-wore sticking to my back.

'Wow, I've heard of the earth moving, but this is taking it a bit too literally …' Rhodri chuckled.

It took me a moment to realise we had begun a slow descent. 'They've got it working!' I exclaimed. Thoughts of being discovered like this, half-dressed and flushed with the glow that comes from good sex, had me scrambling to my feet and hurrying to refasten my bra.

By the time the lift came to a halt on the ground floor, Rhodri and I were just about dressed and looking respectable. I had to stuff my panties and ruined tights into my pocket, and I knew Rhodri had a condom to dispose of at the first opportunity, but when the door opened and Dean trained the camera on us, I was certain no one could guess what we'd been doing while we waited to be rescued.

'Are you both OK?' Dean asked. All I could do was

nod.

The lift engineer wiped his hands on an oily rag. 'Well, I've got it working again, but someone needs to come back in the next couple of days, take a proper look at the thing. In the meantime, I'd recommend you keep the "Out of Order" signs up, just to be on the safe side.'

'Yeah, I'll do that, and I'll ring your office tomorrow, book an appointment.' Rhodri looked at me. 'And we still need to make those security checks.' The tone of his voice made it all too clear that was the last thing he wanted to do.

'Tell you what,' Bayo said, 'I'll make a trip to the nearest all-night garage, get coffee for everyone. I'm sure you're both in need of one after what you've been through.'

'Thanks, mate, much appreciated,' Rhodri said. 'Come on, Jane, let's go look at those fire extinguishers. And this time, we'll take the stairs, OK?'

'OK.'

Once Rhodri had guided me through my duties, he could go home to bed. I would be here for the rest of the night, my mind replaying how it had felt to have sex with him, recalling the scent of his skin, the heat of his kisses, the look of desire and abandon in his eyes as he'd ploughed into me, over and over.

It can't happen again, I told myself firmly. Whatever happens, you can't get involved with a man like Rhodri. But it was useless. Tonight, I'd had a taste of something special, something forbidden but oh so sweet, and I knew that one taste would never be enough.

SEVEN

By the time the woman from the temp agency came to take over the morning shift, I was just about dead on my feet. It was all I could do to wish her a pleasant day before going to collect my things from the locker where I'd left them. At least she'd worked in the Anthony before, so she was familiar with the check-in system. If I'd had to try and explain that to her with my brain fuddled and desperate for sleep, the results would have been disastrous.

Rhodri had gone home for the night once we'd finally completed the security checks. I'd hoped to snatch a word in private with him before he left, but with the camera crew in close attendance that had proved impossible.

I still couldn't quite believe we'd had sex in the lift. In all the time I'd been with Gavin, we'd never once put ourselves in a position where we might get caught in the act, but somehow, that simply added to the thrill. Who knew that danger could be such a turn-on?

More importantly, I needed to reassure myself that nothing had changed between Rhodri and me; that we could continue on a professional footing after everything that had happened. Was he happy for that to have been a one-off, a spur of the moment incident driven by the most bizarre of circumstances? Or did he want more?

His only comment as he'd left had been, 'Goodnight, all. Don't expect to see me too early tomorrow.' He hadn't arrived by the time I came to hand over my shift. I couldn't begrudge him a lie-in for once; he seemed to put in enough unpaid overtime as it was.

Back at the apartment, I took a shower, washing the last remaining traces of Rhodri from my skin. The hot water soothed the deep-seated tension in my muscles, but it did nothing to ease the slight ache between my legs: a delicious reminder of how he had filled and stretched me.

My phone rang as I was putting on my pyjamas. I thought about letting it go to voicemail, then saw Kay's picture on the caller display.

'Hey, darling.' Her tone was cheerful. 'I haven't caught you at a bad time, have I?'

'Actually, I was about to go to bed. I've just got off the night shift at the hotel.'

'Well, in that case, I won't keep you.'

'No, it's OK,' I assured her hastily, 'I'm happy to chat. Though I hope you don't mind if I crawl under the duvet first.'

'That's what Paul always says when he's away on business and I ring him. Hmm, this isn't going to turn into some kind of weird booty call, is it?'

'Kay, much as I love you, I'm just not into women that way.'

'And you're not prepared to make an exception for your best friend?' Kay giggled. 'Paul will be so disappointed. He's always had this fantasy that I'll get it on with another girl ...' She gave me a moment to let the image sink in, and went on, 'So, how are you finding life at the coal face?'

'Hard work. I never thought just sitting at a desk could take so much out of you.'

'Welcome to the real world, darling. But the people you're working with are nice?'

'Yes, they are. The two boys in the camera crew are great; I get on really well with them. And the staff at the hotel have made me feel more welcome than I thought they would. They all genuinely believe that I'm here trying to get work experience in the industry, and they're doing their best to help me.'

'I'm sure they are, but what I really want to know is whether you've met anyone you might be interested in getting to know a little better?'

'Well …' I twisted a lock of hair between my fingers, wondering whether I should say anything. 'The manager is pretty cute.'

'Ooh, do tell! What's he like?'

He's amazing, I wanted to say. He's got muscles in all the right places, a gorgeous, thick cock, and when he comes, he makes this odd little grunting sound in his throat. But I gave her the PG-rated version, thinking it wiser not to reveal that I'd let him fuck me up against the wall in a broken-down lift. 'His name's Rhodri, he's from Aberpentre, and he's got the most beautiful blue eyes. But like I told you, Kay, I'm not looking to get involved with anyone.'

'Oh, you say that, but honestly, you need to live a little.'

I went to reply, about to tell her it wasn't easy living at all when I had a camera trained on my every move, but my words came out as a yawn.

'Claudia, I can see I'm keeping you up. I'll ring you back for a proper chat. When's a good time to catch you?'

'Well, I go on shift at midnight, so you could try me some time this evening.'

'Tonight's not going to be possible, sorry. Paul and I have got tickets for *Death of a Salesman* at the Old Vic. It's got that actor out of *The Wire* in the lead role. You know the one I mean. Oh, what's his name …?'

'Well, enjoy it, and I'll speak to you later in the week. And don't worry about me, or my love life. We'll be just fine, I promise.'

I fell asleep with the phone still clutched in my hand.

When I woke, it was early evening. Fuzzy headed and lethargic, I staggered to the kitchen and put the kettle on. Gazing out of the window, I looked at the pale blue waters of the bay without really seeing them. I consoled myself that this change to my regular routine would only last a week. How did those who worked a rotating shift pattern cope? Did their body clocks eventually adjust, or did they stumble around like zombies the whole time, just as I was doing now?

Having brewed a mug of strong tea, I took it into the lounge, where I powered up my laptop. It had been a while since I'd checked my emails. Having quickly ascertained there was nothing of any immediate importance waiting for me at work, I turned to my personal account. A couple of jokes forwarded to me by Kay, an invitation to the opening of an art exhibition in Camden, curated by a friend of a friend, a reminder that the licence on my anti-virus software would shortly be due for renewal …

Then I remembered the account that I'd set up at the

request of the Wild Card production team. Jane had needed an email address for the fake CV that had been sent over to Rhodri, so I'd created one on her behalf. I rarely bothered to look at it, having done little more than send test messages to check the address functioned, and once filming was completed I'd be able to delete it altogether. But now I logged in, and found a message from Rhodri waiting in the inbox.

Hi Jane,

Just wanted to check that you were OK after last night. Sorry I didn't get the chance to speak to you properly before I left, but I was shattered. It was kind of a long, strange day. But you need to know there's no one I'd rather be stuck in a lift with. Maybe we can do it again sometime ☺

Rhodri x

Smiling, I rattled off a reply.

Hi Rhodri,

Everything's fine here – I just rolled out of bed, so sorry for not getting back to you sooner. Told you I wasn't used to working nights ☺ It was all very quiet after you left – let's hope it stays the same for the rest of the week. I'll be taking the stairs because I think it's safer that way, but I'm sure we could get stuck somewhere else if we wanted ...

Jane xx

Only after I'd pressed "send" did I worry that might be an inappropriate response to offer my boss. But I couldn't call it back now.

From the bedroom came the sound of the phone warbling. I thought about not answering it, then realised Kay might have been able to find a few minutes in her schedule to ring me back.

I dashed to retrieve the phone from beneath my duvet. When I answered it, a voice I hadn't expected to hear said, 'Just got out of bed, eh? So what are you wearing, exactly?'

'Mr Wynn-Jones,' I replied with mock primness, 'what kind of question is that to be asking a member of your staff?'

'Hey, Jane, you know you can't plant an image in a man's mind and just leave it at that. We're visual creatures. We need more in the way of detail.'

'If you must know, I'm in a pair of pyjamas with little polka dots on them.'

'And I'm sure you look very nice in them.' He lowered his voice. 'But I bet you'd look even nicer out of them …'

'Seriously, Rhodri, did you ring me up just to talk dirty?'

'Well, that wasn't the intention at first. Like I said in my email, I wanted to make sure you got through the rest of your shift OK – I mean, you did get a bit freaked out when the lift broke down. But then I started remembering all the things we did, and how good you felt in my arms, and how I never got to tell you how incredible you were.'

So did this mean he felt the same way I did? He'd been thinking about last night, thinking about us together … I got on the bed and lay on my back, looking up at the ceiling. 'Are you still in the office?'

'No, I left about twenty minutes ago. I just got home and decided to check my emails before I had a shower, and I saw your message.'

'So if you were just about to get in the shower, maybe I should be asking you what you're wearing?'

He chuckled, clearly amused that I'd thrown his own question back at him. 'I'm still in my suit. Haven't even taken my tie off.'

His words brought back the fantasy I'd conjured up the other night: Rhodri, stripping for me and obeying my every command. 'So do it. Take off your tie, and your footwear, and let me know you're doing it.'

For a moment, there was silence, and I wondered whether I'd pushed him too far. But his voice came back on the line. 'OK, I'm going to get out of my shoes, but I'm going to have to sit down, otherwise this might get a bit awkward ...' I heard rustling noises, and then a bump, as if he'd thrown one of his shoes across the room. The second quickly followed, while I tried to imagine the scene.

'Are you in your bedroom?' I asked him.

'No, the living room. I'm looking out of my window at the woods behind my home ...'

'Well, stop admiring the view and keep undressing.' There was a snap to my voice; the tone I usually reserved for making a point in board meetings, when I needed to remind the rest of the people in the room who was boss. I'd never used that tone on Rhodri – wouldn't dream of addressing him in that way under any other circumstances – but it got the desired reaction.

'Yes, ma'am.'

'Ma'am,' I murmured, half to myself. His sudden deference caused a rush of liquid heat to flood through me. 'I like that.'

'My socks are off,' Rhodri announced. 'And my tie.'

'Lose the jacket.'

This time, he didn't question the instruction, or employ any delaying tactics. I pictured him peeling the jacket off his shoulders, and placing it over the back of a chair, just as he did in his office. Absent-mindedly, I ran the pad of my thumb over my nipple, the thick cotton of my pyjama top doing little to dull the sensation that prickled in the tight bud.

'How are you doing, Rhodri?'

'I'm out of the jacket, ma'am. And ... my trousers are starting to get a little tight.'

His words had me picturing the bulge at his crotch, straining against his fly. I could almost see him pulling down the zip, reaching in to free his cock, and I bit my lip to stop a whimper escaping. It wouldn't do to make him aware of my need for him. I had to remain in control of this scene, in control of myself.

'The trousers can wait,' I told him. 'I want you to take off your shirt first.'

'Of course. Whatever the lady wants ...'

While I listened to the sounds of Rhodri fumbling with buttons, I slipped my hand under the edge of my top, and caressed my breasts. If only it could be Rhodri cupping and squeezing them, just as he'd done in the lift. I could still feel the burn of his stubble, rasping across the soft flesh as he buried his face in my cleavage.

'How are you doing?' I asked, hearing him utter a muffled curse as he fought to free his arm from one of the

100

sleeves.

'Fine … almost there. But don't you think this is just a little bit one-sided?'

I feigned ignorance. 'How do you mean?'

'Well, I'm standing here half-naked, and you haven't taken anything off yet. Isn't it about time we evened this up a bit?'

I couldn't resist testing the boundaries, seeing quite how far I could push him in my role as the dominant mistress. 'Rhodri, remember who's in charge here …'

'And maybe you should remember who's in charge the rest of the time. How would you like to go back to being part of Wioletta's housekeeping team?'

'You wouldn't dare!'

'Oh, don't you try me, missy. Scrubbing toilets would only be the beginning. You've no idea what I'd dare to do if I was with you right now.'

I squirmed against the bedcovers. 'Tell me.'

'I'd put you over my knee, pull down those pyjama bottoms and give you a good spanking …'

Now I couldn't prevent an excited little noise slipping from my mouth. Just the thought of Rhodri swatting my bare bum with his big, capable hands had me pushing a hand into my pyjama bottoms.

'Go on, Jane. Take your top off.'

Continuing to refuse might be fun, just to find out how Rhodri would respond, but by now, I wanted to be naked for him. 'I'm doing it,' I told him. As each button came undone, I gave him a running commentary. 'It's open halfway … Now I've reached the last button … If you were here right now, you'd be able to see my nipples, see how pink and stiff they are. You'd be able to take them in

101

your mouth, just like you did last night.'

On the other end of the line, I heard him groan, and I shivered at the strength of his reaction to my words.

'Undressing for you is turning me on so much, Rhodri. Is it turning you on?'

'Yes, ma'am.' Now his tone was hushed, reverent.

'Are you hard? Do you want to touch yourself?'

'Oh, God, yes …'

'Then go ahead. Play with that big, gorgeous cock of yours. But don't undo your trousers; just stroke yourself through them.'

Silence stretched out for so long, I began to think I'd pushed Rhodri a step too far and he'd put the phone down on me. Then I heard a hiss of breath, and knew he was reacting to the feel of his own fingers. How frustrating must it be, to have those caresses dulled by the fabric of his suit trousers when he really wanted to take himself properly in hand.

'Is that good, Rhodri?'

I had to strain to hear his reply. 'Oh, yes …'

'Would it be better if you had your hot, hard shaft in your hand?'

'Fuck, Jane, keep talking like that and I'm going to come. I can't hold back any longer.'

'Then you have my permission to take everything off.'

I thought he might demand something from me in return; ask that I get naked too. But by now, it seemed the only thought in Rhodri's mind was his swiftly approaching orgasm. Holding the phone in one hand so I could listen to the sounds of him scrabbling out of his clothes, I used the other to ease my pyjama bottoms down until I could kick them off.

'Rhodri,' I murmured, once I was assured that he'd obeyed my command, 'I've bared myself for you, too.'

'You filthy little minx,' he said. I'd never been called that before, but I liked it. It made me sound deliciously cunning and committed to pleasure – his, as well as mine.

'That's how turned on you get me,' I told him, 'and I wish you were here now, to lick me where I need it the most. Just think how good I'd taste.'

Rhodri lost the last, tenuous grasp on his control, moaning out the word, 'Coming.'

That was all it took to have me crying out in my own pleasure, my velvet walls clutching tight around my fingers. For a moment, all I could hear was the fierce pounding of my heart. Then, as I sought to catch my breath, Rhodri spoke down the phone line to me. 'Hey, Jane, are you still there?'

'Mm-hm.' I sprawled back against the bedcovers, staring at the coving on the ceiling as it came slowly back into focus.

'You're incredible, you know that? But the next time you come, it's going to be on my command.'

Bold words indeed, but I had no doubt he meant them. I was still smiling when I ended the call and let the phone drop from my nerveless fingers.

EIGHT

'Working on the night shift ...' I tapped the ballpoint pen against the desktop, ordering my thoughts. Speaking softly so my voice didn't echo around the empty lobby, I continued, 'It's taken some getting used to, I'll admit. I'm sure it becomes easier if you're doing it week in, week out, but I really need to speak to the other receptionists, and see how they cope with the rotating shift patterns. Maybe the manager should be looking at having a dedicated night duty receptionist here, so the other members of staff aren't constantly being asked to change their routine.'

This wasn't the first time I'd felt the urge to confess all into my little digital video camera since I'd started covering Morwenna's shift. Having no one else to speak to for hours on end would do that to a person.

Every night, I paced the hotel corridors, carrying out all the required security checks. Once I'd assured myself that none of the fire doors was obstructed, the extinguishers were all in their little cubby holes at the top of each flight of stairs, and the staff cloakroom was clean and tidy, I would settle down at the front desk with a book of Sudoku puzzles. Forcing myself to concentrate on fitting the numbers into their correct position on each grid helped keep me awake through the small hours.

Despite the comments both Rhodri and Bayo had made about the hotel being a haven for ghostly goings-on, it wasn't the odd creaking floorboard or sudden flickering of the lights that unsettled me. It was the stillness, and the absence of company. Usually, by one in the morning the last of the guests had wandered in from an evening spent in Aberpentre's pubs and clubs, wishing me a tired, slightly slurred goodnight as they crossed the lobby. As the minutes ticked slowly by, I knew I had to be the only person left awake in the entire hotel.

Not even a slight rumble of traffic came from the road outside; only the low hum of the heating system and the scratching of my pen on the pages of the Sudoku book broke the silence. I would find myself gazing at the switchboard, hoping to see the blinking light that meant someone was ringing down from one of the rooms, needing assistance. Even if they had a problem that couldn't be solved until the morning, when Owen and his trusty toolbox came back on duty, the sound of their voice would have broken the monotony of my shift.

After the sheer madness of that first night, and the exhilaration of being trapped in the lift with Rhodri, I should have welcomed the peace and quiet. But instead, it caused my mind to race. I caught myself thinking back to the way he had lifted me up in his strong arms, so I could impale myself on his cock: the steady, piston-like action of that thick length as it thrust up into me. I replayed over and again the phone sex we'd shared, every last, gloriously dirty word burned into my memory. And I wished, more than anything, that we could build on those moments, creating something strong enough to last for more than just the few weeks of my undercover stint in the hotel.

That last thought, I knew, was ridiculous. As far as Rhodri was concerned, I was Jane Ennis, flat broke and down on my luck, desperate enough for a way to rebuild my life that I would let a documentary film crew follow my every move. When he learnt the truth – that I owned the company for which he worked, and had the power to shape the future of this hotel, and all the others in the chain – he would never be able to see me in the same way.

So I'd done my best to stop thinking about Rhodri, and started thinking instead about the decisions I would have to make once I returned to London. To that end, I'd made a list of all the pros and cons involved in keeping the Aberpentre Anthony, as opposed to selling it. At the moment – and that list was currently tucked between the pages of my Sudoku book, in case I needed to add to it – the cons still outweighed the pros. Try as I might to think about all its good points, like its old-fashioned charm and its committed, hard-working staff, I could only see an outdated building, seriously in need of renovation, that continued to be a drain on our bottom line. Dad had warned me that I'd have to make some tough decisions when I eventually became CEO. Getting rid of this hotel would be one of the most difficult, but the longer I spent here, despite all my hopes that its fortunes could be revived, the more necessary it seemed.

Even harder would be persuading Rhodri to remain within the company. Leaving my personal feelings aside, I viewed him as an important asset from a business point of view. There would be openings for him, the chance to manage bigger and better hotels than this, and from what he'd told me, he had no qualms about leaving his hometown behind to further his prospects. But I needed to have that conversation with him as Claudia, not Jane, and I had no idea how he'd react to that.

Turning back to the camera, I said, 'I didn't realise when I decided to take part in this programme that I'd learn things about myself, as well as the running of the business. But being here is making me reassess what I want from life, just as much as what I need and expect from my staff, so perhaps this experiment has been more worthwhile than I thought.' I chewed on the end of the pen for a moment. 'Of course, I'll have a better idea of all this once I'm back in the office ... back as myself. I'm enjoying my time as Jane, don't get me wrong, but it'll be nice to return to being Claudia again.'

Now, for Rhodri's sake as well as my own, I just had to figure out where Jane ended and Claudia began.

Working nights meant I had to change my routine in any number of ways I hadn't considered at first. When I came off my shift, exhausted from hours of doing nothing, I just wanted to sleep. My early-morning jogs had become a thing of the past, and when I woke in mid-afternoon, the sea front was too crowded with holidaymakers to make running practical. I had no wish to become one of those self-important fitness freaks who expects other people to dive out of their way as they pound the pavement.

Instead, I would roll out a small mat on my living room floor and go through a series of yoga poses. They might not be helping me achieve the serenity and inner peace that Drew, the instructor at my local gym, promised was a side benefit of his classes. But it felt good to stretch my muscles as I moved from the upward dog into a forward fold, clearing my mind of all thoughts and concentrating on a simple internal mantra.

I bow to the sun, and ask for enlightenment.

However many times I repeated the words, I knew that enlightenment would be a long time coming.

It didn't help that I hadn't seen as much of Rhodri as I'd like. Most mornings, I'd left the hotel before he arrived. I might have thought he was avoiding me if I hadn't been aware that was his usual work pattern. Moreover, on the one occasion he had bumped into me in the corridor when I'd been collecting my bag from the locker, he'd pushed me up against the wall and whispered in my ear, 'Don't forget, Jane. On my command.'

Immediately, my thoughts had flashed back to our intimate phone conversation the other night, and his promise that he would take control of my next orgasm. The desire blazing in his eyes left me in no doubt he was serious, and I couldn't help wondering when and where he might decide to turn those words into actions.

He'd pressed a kiss to my lips that left me breathless and hungry for more. Then we'd heard footsteps approaching down the corridor, and pulled apart before anyone could catch us in the act. He knew the consequences of discovery as well as I did.

'Sleep well, Jane, and sweet dreams,' had been his parting words to me. He must have known those dreams would all be of him.

I was still thinking about that stolen kiss when my phone buzzed and Kay's image appeared on the screen.

'Hi, stranger,' I greeted her. 'How was your play the other night?'

'Absolutely gripping. It must have been good; Paul managed to stay awake through the whole thing.'

She gave a little laugh. Paul's ability to fall asleep no matter where he might be was legendary. He'd once nodded off leaning on the railing by the finish line at Epsom racecourse, oblivious to the horses thundering past.

'And we've discovered this fantastic little restaurant on the South Bank,' she went on. 'It's run by a guy who won *Masterchef* a couple of years ago, and he cooks the most amazing Japanese fusion dishes. I never knew sea urchin could taste so delicious ...'

'Well, I'm glad to know you're surviving OK without me.'

'What about you? Has your wicked boss still got you working nights?'

'Yes, but it's only until the end of the week. And anyway, Rhodri's not wicked.'

'No, from what I recall you seemed to think he was quite a cutie ...'

I sighed, knowing Kay had no intention to let the subject drop. 'OK, yes, he's a good-looking boy. But that's all I'm doing, I promise you, looking.'

And listening ... But she didn't need to know about all the intimate things Rhodri had said to me over the phone, and just how hot and heavy things had got between us.

'Well, it's nice to know you're at least taking that much of an interest in a man again. I was starting to think you'd given them up for good.'

'How do you know I haven't?' I walked into the kitchen, and started filling the kettle with the phone

110

perched in the crook between my neck and my shoulder. If Kay was intending to settle in for a long conversation, I needed coffee to accompany it. 'Anyway, I'm not here to try and find a man. I'm here to try and find out why we have one hotel in our chain which is doing so much worse than all the rest.'

The passion in my voice must have been obvious to Kay. 'Does it really matter? I mean, didn't you say your dad was seriously contemplating selling the place? That suggests he didn't want it to be his problem any longer.'

'I did, but I look around the hotel and I can't believe he'd allowed it to fall into quite such a state of disrepair. Dad always took such pride in the properties he owned, but everything here is just so … shabby. And the lift is a real museum piece. It should have been taken out and replaced years ago.'

Behind me, the kettle came to a noisy boil. I went over to the fridge, and retrieved the ground coffee I kept in there. The distinct aroma of hazelnuts hit my nostrils as I opened the package. For all its faults, the town had one decent Italian deli, which meant I'd been able to treat myself to my favourite of all the flavoured blends.

'And is it worth hanging on to, if you were to sort out everything that's wrong with it?' Kay said.

Spooning coffee into the cafetière, I considered her question. 'Honestly? I'm not sure. I mean, this isn't the prettiest town I've ever spent time in, but the hotel would be a good base to explore the local coastline and all the sites of interest nearby.' I thought of Castell Aberpentre, and the thousand years of history contained in its ruined walls. 'It's just whether we could recoup the serious investment we'd need to make in order to bring the place up to the required standard. But I shouldn't be boring you with all this, Kay; it's not your problem.'

'Don't worry about it. You know you can always use me as a sounding board.'

How many times in the months since Dad died had I found myself talking out some issue or other over lunch with Kay, a glass of Merlot at hand to aid with the thinking process? 'Thanks, but I'm trying not to think about work at the moment.'

'So let's talk about cute men instead ...' Kay seemed about to add something else, then said, 'Oh, there's someone at the front door. Must be the man with the grocery delivery I'm expecting. Sorry, darling, but I'm going to have to love you and leave you.'

After Kay had ended the call, I stood for a while staring at nothing. Something she'd said still nagged at me. She'd mentioned Dad "contemplating" the sale of the Anthony here in Aberpentre. He'd gone beyond mere contemplation: as far as I knew, there had been a serious offer on the table at the time of his death. I needed to know what kind of figures had been discussed, and what value had been placed on the property. It would help me with the difficult decisions I had to make regarding the hotel.

Taking my coffee through to the living room, I set the mug down on the table, and brought my laptop out of "sleep" mode. Here was where I kept various files I had transferred from the PC in Dad's home office: files that had been intended for his eyes alone. I'd cracked the password on his computer at the initial attempt – "Jacqueline", my mother's name. Even a dozen years after he had lost her to ovarian cancer, she had still been the first thing on his mind.

Scrolling through various folders, I found one marked "ABERPENTRE". Opening the first document, I discovered it contained the basic specifications of the hotel – number of rooms, facilities, the level of staff needed to maintain it. Pretty much all of this was information I knew from first-hand experience. There were also copies of the business accounts for the last five years. It came as no surprise to me to see that every year, the losses mounted, although the hotel was still just about breaking even.

Of more immediate interest was the series of emails that had been exchanged by my father and Alastair Hammond of Golden State Properties, the man who'd been interested in taking the Anthony off his hands. As I read through the correspondence, it became increasingly obvious that Hammond's interest lay not in keeping the hotel as a going concern. Instead, he intended to redevelop it, turning it into a luxury apartment complex, complete with gym and leisure facilities including a sauna and swimming pool.

Who on earth, I wondered, would want to build expensive flats in a rundown little resort like Aberpentre? In a city like Cardiff, where the derelict docklands along the bay had been turned into a spectacular collection of offices, restaurants, and living spaces, it might have made sense, but not here …

Unpleasant possibilities flashed through my mind, as I remembered some scheme a banker friend of Gavin's had been involved with. I couldn't remember all the details – I'd tried very hard not to listen when Gavin was detailing all the ways in which he had dreams of spending my

113

money – but the man had apparently invested in some equally unlikely property scheme as a way of writing off money against tax. However, I refused to believe that Dad would have been involved in anything illegal. Though his business rivals might have seen it as a weakness, he'd always retained his principles.

Reading on, I discovered a legitimate reason lay behind Hammond's eagerness to buy the hotel. A European regeneration grant had been awarded that would see new, hi-tech businesses being attracted to this part of the Llŷn Peninsula. A rash of well-paying jobs would be created in the software industry, attracting people who would snap up the luxury seafront apartments Golden State intended to build.

The information should have put my mind at rest, but something still didn't feel right. I looked again at the sum Hammond had been offering Dad. If the figures quoted were correct – and I had no reason to doubt them – what Hammond was prepared to pay seemed way above any serious market valuation, even with the potential for making a killing on the sale of the apartments he envisaged. I might have understood it if there had been interest from other competing parties, but I couldn't see any evidence that anyone else wanted to buy the hotel.

I'd have had my concerns if my father had been willing to accept a sum that was way below the Anthony's true worth, but somehow the property developer's generosity set the same alarm bells ringing. Maybe Dad had believed he was fleecing some naïve American who'd misjudged the exchange rate, but from their correspondence, Alastair Hammond appeared to be a very shrewd operator. It didn't add up.

The wording on the page began to blur, and I rubbed at my eyes. Why hadn't Dad trusted me enough to share any of this information with me while he was still alive? I closed the files and powered down the laptop. When I returned to London, perhaps I should get in touch with Alastair Hammond. I needed to find out whether he showed any interest in rekindling these negotiations, and what value he placed on the hotel now, given how much the property market had picked up in the last year. If so, he would discover that Gus Anthony's daughter was prepared to drive just as hard a bargain as her father would have done.

NINE

The only sour note in my week of night duty came in the early hours of Sunday morning. It was gone two o'clock when a couple of lights started blinking on the switchboard, both belonging to rooms on the third floor. I answered each call in turn, only to receive the same complaint: noise from their neighbours in Room 304 had woken them, and though they had tried banging on the door – and in one case, the adjoining wall – the banging and screaming had continued. Could I do something, *anything*, to try and get them to calm down?

If Dean had been around, he and his camera would already be on his way up to the scene of the disturbance. But he wasn't due back from Chester until tomorrow lunchtime, so I was on my own. It's probably for the best, I told myself as I put the phone down on the woman from Room 306, having assured her that I was on my way to sort out the problem. After all, I have absolutely no idea what I'm going to find up there.

I took the stairs, even though the lift had received a thorough inspection and was now in full working order once more. Sometimes, you just don't want to tempt fate.

By the time I reached Room 304, it seemed like the

occupants of half the rooms on the floor had been woken by the commotion, and were poking their heads out of their doors, eager to discover what was happening.

The women who'd called me from Room 306 stood in her doorway, huddled in a floral-patterned silk wrap. 'There's someone yelling bloody murder in there,' she informed me. 'And they have no respect for the fact people are trying to sleep. Maybe you should have called the police.'

I nodded at her. 'Don't worry; I'm sure we'll be able to resolve things without having to get them involved.' Taking a deep breath, I knocked sharply on the door. 'Mr Smith –' I'd checked the name under which the room had been booked before I'd come upstairs, grateful that for once I'd been able to retrieve the information without the computer system crashing. All I received in reply was what sounded like something heavy being thrown, followed by a distinct cry of pain.

'Mr Hammond, is everything OK in there?'

A woman's voice was raised in response. Even though the words were muffled by the thick wood, the tone was distinctly unfriendly. The sound of male sobbing that accompanied her words proved more alarming. Not giving myself time to worry whether I was doing the right thing, I took the master key card from my jacket pocket. Rhodri had told me that the front desk staff were only supposed to let themselves into a guest's room in an emergency. Well, if this didn't count as an emergency, I had no idea what did.

I don't know what I expected to see when I opened the door, but it certainly wasn't the sight that greeted me. A man knelt on the bed, wearing nothing but a pair of stockings attached to a frilly, black suspender belt that strained around his portly waist. He appeared to be handcuffed to the slatted headboard, and his mouth was firmly gagged. Beside him stood a woman with peroxide blonde hair, her already impressive height boosted to well over six feet by a pair of stiletto-heeled thigh boots. Her breasts, so big and round they had to be surgically enhanced, threatened to spill from the cups of a scarlet and black corset. The black rubber table tennis bat she clutched and the vivid red blotches on the man's bare backside explained the source of the anguished cries the guests in the neighbouring rooms and I had heard.

'What the hell –?' the blonde snapped in a thick Scouse accent.

I hoped my shock didn't register on my face. 'I'm terribly sorry to intrude on you like this, Mr and – er – Mrs Smith.' Already, I was beginning to think the couple might not have booked in under their real names. 'It's just that the people next door heard a lot of noise coming from your room, and they were – um – concerned that someone might be in pain.'

'Look, love, if he's not in pain then I'm not doing my job properly …'

The man on the bed was grunting from behind his gag, trying to attract his partner's attention. When that didn't work, he let drop something he'd been clutching in his bunched fist. It landed on the floor with a tinkling of bells, and I realised with a mixture of shock and amusement it was one of those little plastic balls that are thrown for dogs and cats to chase. This scene was growing more surreal by the moment, and I was increasingly glad Dean wasn't here to film it.

Dropping the ball seemed to act as some kind of signal, and the blonde hurried to release the man from his bondage. When she unbuckled the gag from around his face, he cleared his throat and said, 'I'm terribly sorry, Miss ...'

'Please, call me Jane,' I said, still feeling distinctly uncomfortable under the blonde's icy glare.

He rose to a kneeling position, pulling the bedcovers hastily around him, but not before I'd caught a glimpse of his half-hard cock. 'Jane. Ruby and I didn't realise we were disturbing the other guests. Could you offer them our most sincere apologies?'

I nodded, hoping this would resolve the situation to everyone's satisfaction. 'Of course, but I think everyone would appreciate it if you kept the noise down for the rest of the night.'

'Absolutely.'

As I left the room, I heard the blonde say, 'You'll be for it when I get you home.'

'Oh,' he replied eagerly, 'I do hope so, mistress.'

I pulled the door shut behind me, and leant against it for a moment. Tomorrow, I'd be able to laugh about this, but now I had angry guests to placate.

'So,' the woman from Room 306 said, 'what on earth was happening in there?'

'Oh, nothing serious,' I assured her. 'They were just working on some kinks in their relationship ... Anyway, they wanted me to let you know that they're very sorry to have disturbed you, and it's not going to happen again.'

She nodded. 'Thank you for stepping in.'

'It's all part of the service. And I do hope what happened tonight won't put you off staying at our hotels in future.'

With a small nod and a quiet, 'Goodnight,' she retreated into her room. The excitement over, the other guests had begun to shut their own doors.

I walked back down to the reception area, mulling over the night's events in my mind. Part of me wanted to tell Rhodri what had happened, to prove to him that Jane could cope with whatever bizarre situation arose in his absence. But I doubted I'd see him till Monday, when I was back on the morning shift. And I couldn't make one of my video confessions about what I'd seen. Amusing as it would be to describe how I'd walked in on a couple acting out a mistress and slave game, if Hugo Murray saw the footage, he'd want to know why Dean hadn't been around to film the incident. We could lie, and tell him the couple had refused to sign the release form that would allow any footage in which they appeared to be included in the documentary, but I didn't want to run the risk of Hugo finding out that one of his employees had been in Chester visiting his boyfriend when he should have been working.

More than that, I didn't think the pair had been doing anything that warranted them being presented as some kind of freak show on TV, which I knew was the angle the show's editor would take. They'd been inconsiderate enough to wake their neighbours – and maybe that would make them think twice the next time they chose their destination for a dirty weekend – but Mr Smith had been genuinely apologetic when he realised the nuisance they'd caused. Still, it would teach me not to wish for something to liven up my boring shifts. It would be a long time before I stopped seeing the marks that paddle had left on Mr Smith's soundly beaten arse.

The banging on the door was insistent, but this time someone was trying to attract my attention. I'd just settled on the sofa with a cup of coffee, and I didn't need anything to disturb me. I'd found one of the Freeview channels showing back-to-back episodes of *Come Dine with Me*; perfect viewing for a rainy Sunday afternoon. The rest of my shift had been quiet, but I hadn't slept well once I'd got home. I'd been disturbed by dreams in which I was handcuffed to a bed, half-naked, and Rhodri was beating my bottom with a sturdy paddle. They'd been so vivid that when I'd woken, I'd had to slip a hand between my legs and bring myself to the peak of pleasure. Now, I just wanted to veg out and enjoy some quiet time to myself.

'Hey, Jane, are you in there?' Dean's voice. Wanting to ignore him but knowing I couldn't, I went to open the door. Maybe he just wanted to chat about his visit to Chester, and Maurice, but his timing could have been better.

'Hi, Dean, what can I do for you?'

'Oh.' He looked me up and down. 'I thought you'd be ready to go by now.'

In my grey marl T-shirt and dotty pyjama bottoms, and with my hair swathed in a towel to aid with the deep conditioning treatment I'd applied, I couldn't have been less ready to go anywhere.

'What are you talking about?'

'Didn't you get the message I sent?' When I shook my head, he muttered, 'I really need to check I've got the correct phone number for you. Well, I need you to get dressed, sharpish. We've got some filming to do.'

'Filming?' My heart sank. 'But Dean, I've been at work

till eight this morning. I need some "me time".'

'No such thing on this project, I'm afraid. Especially not when the weather's perfect for what I have in mind.'

'Perfect? It's pouring down with rain.'

'Exactly. I've been asked to get some shots of you we can run beneath the voiceover when the programme comes back from an ad break, reminding the viewers who you are, and why you're in Aberpentre. They need to know that the hotel is failing because no one's coming here on holiday any more, and nothing will say that better than a sequence of you walking along a deserted promenade in the rain.'

'This is one of Hugo's ideas, isn't it?'

'No, but it's just the sort of footage he loves. The man's nothing if not predictable, but his shows do win a lot of National TV Awards. Now, chop-chop, babe, we haven't got all day …'

Dean stood with his hands on his hips, his expression expectant. I shrugged, and headed for the bathroom, pulling the towel from my head as I went.

Within fifteen minutes, I'd rinsed and rough-dried my hair, changed into jeans and a stripy Breton-style top and applied a little make-up. My mood hadn't brightened, but at least Dean seemed pleased with the effort I'd put in.

'Very nice. Come on, let's go downstairs and collect Bayo.'

After I'd grabbed my coat and bag, we left the apartment. With a brief stop-off on the floor below so Bayo could join us, we headed out into the rain-washed car park.

As I looked in the direction of the deserted beach and the flat, grey sea, I thought back to the night I'd arrived in

Aberpentre. The weather had been just as dismal then. So much had changed in the intervening fortnight, not least in the relationship between Rhodri and me, but the resort retained a bleak, depressing air. Exactly what Dean hoped to capture on film.

'So, what, you just want me to walk along the sea front for a bit?' I asked him, by way of clarification.

'Well, I was thinking about that when you were getting changed. I thought we could also go up to Castell Aberpentre. That way, I'll have some nice, moody footage of you walking around the ruins of the castle, but it'll also give me the opportunity to get some establishing views of the bay and the hotel. I'm afraid the Wild Card budget doesn't quite stretch to aerial footage.'

'And that's why he's roped me in.' Bayo spoke with the tone of someone who, like me, would rather have had his feet up in front of the TV. 'He doesn't need me for the sound, but I'm the one who does all the driving.'

Dean turned the collar of his denim jacket up against the rain. 'Are we going to stand round all day, or are we going to get on with this? The sooner we start, the sooner you two moaning Minnies will be back inside.'

We let ourselves into Bayo's car. He tuned the radio to a station playing classic oldies from the 1980s, and we set off in the direction of the castle on the hill. From reading the leaflets in the hotel lobby, I knew the ruins were maintained by the local council and the site was free to visit. Presumably, that was another part of the reasoning behind Dean's decision to film there. If he'd had to deal with a property that belonged to English Heritage or the National Trust, the staff might not have been willing to

124

deal with his request.

The car park at the bottom of the cliff face, big enough to accommodate half a dozen vehicles, was empty. Bayo turned off the engine and sat for a moment, looking up at the steep path to the top.

'You know,' he said reflectively, 'there's really no need for me to go all that way up there with you. I may as well just sit here and wait till you're done filming.'

Dean shook his head. 'No way, mate. What have you been doing the past couple of days while I've been away? Festering in the apartment with that games console of yours, I'll bet. You need some exercise, and the walk will do you good.'

'Is he always this bossy?' I asked Bayo, as we began our steady ascent towards the castle.

'Yeah, but I don't mind, really. I've never got on with anyone I've worked with as well as I do with Dean, even if he does get a bit mother hen at times.'

Dean strode on ahead of us, making light work of the climb despite having to carry his camera. As the path wound round the hill, the castle loomed up directly above us. If I'd been one of Edward I's forces, would I have paused in my march up the hill, awed by the great, fortified towers, and wondered if I was doing the right thing? No doubt arrows and other missiles would have been raining down on me from the narrow windows of the fortress, enough to make any sane man want to turn and flee. Maybe they'd even have had boiling oil poured on them. I was glad the worst we had to contend with was the rain, which by now had slowed to a slight but persistent drizzle.

'Magnificent, isn't it?' Dean commented, as Bayo and I

joined him in front of the castle's gatehouse. 'Just imagine what it would have been like before half of it was destroyed.'

'I can see why they chose to build on this hill,' Bayo said, looking back down the way we'd come. 'You've got a view for miles in every direction, you can have supplies brought to you by sea as well as by land, and you could have lit beacons here and used the place as an early warning system if anyone tried to invade.'

'See, and if you'd stayed in the car, you would have never got to appreciate any of that,' Dean pointed out.

'Please, you two … You're like an old married couple.' I sighed. 'So Dean, what do you need me to do?'

'Oh, just walk round the site, maybe stand and look out to sea for a while. I'll let you know when I'm happy, and then I'll just get the shots I need of the town and the bay.'

I did as he asked; running my fingers over the pitted, fire-scarred walls and trying to imagine what it might have been like to live within them. Would I have been a simple serving girl, or would I have been the lady of the castle, attended by my many brave and loyal knights? The bravest of all would have been Sir Rhodri. I pictured him in simple chainmail, his hair blowing wildly about his face as he stood on the ramparts, sword in hand, ready to repel any invader at my bidding …

When I turned, and looked out over the town below us, the Anthony Hotel stood out, even from this distance. Just like the castle, it had been designed to draw the eye, and to make a statement about the wealth and status of those who resided there.

Lost in thought, I vaguely heard Dean say, 'OK, that's it, thank you,' and I wandered back to stand with Bayo while Dean finished filming. At last, he seemed satisfied he had everything he needed, and we made our way back to the car.

'There, that wasn't too painful, was it?' he said.

Even less painful, but far more boring, were the ten minutes he spent making me walk along the promenade, and down onto the beach and back, much to the interest of a handful of passers-by, who stopped just long enough to work out whether or not someone famous was being filmed before moving on.

Finally, Dean appeared to have all the footage Hugo and his editors could want. 'I don't know about you,' he said as he packed away his camera, 'but all this sea air has given me a real appetite. Why don't we go get some fish and chips?'

Bayo beamed broadly. 'Now that's the best idea you've had all day.'

We crossed the road to the Aberpentre Fish Bar, and joined the queue waiting for the girl behind the counter to dredge a fresh batch of fish out of the fryer. Dean ordered three portions of cod and chips, and when everything was ready, the girl heaped chips onto three polystyrene trays that she'd placed on greaseproof paper, before topping each one with a battered fish.

'This looks fantastic,' Dean said, shaking salt and vinegar liberally over his chips. There wasn't room in the little shop to sit and eat our food, but a couple of wooden trestle tables stood on the forecourt, protected from the drizzle by a black and white striped awning.

We spread our parcels of food out on one of the tables, and tucked in. I hadn't realised how hungry I was till I popped the first golden, perfectly crunchy chip into my mouth.

'When I was a kid, this was the best thing about going to the seaside.' Bayo waved a half-eaten chip in the air to emphasise his point. 'Never mind the paddling and the donkey rides. Every summer we used to have a week's holiday in Scarborough, and we'd always go off to Whitby for the day, just so my dad could go to this little café that does the best fish and chips in the world ...'

'Maurice and I went to Whitby a couple of years ago,' Dean said. 'He'd just landed the part of Jonathan Harker in the musical version of *Dracula*, so we went there to do some research.'

'Research? How so?' I forked up another mouthful of white, flaky cod.

'Bram Stoker was fascinated with the town, and with the ruined abbey in particular, and he set part of the novel there. It's where Count Dracula's boat is washed ashore when he comes to England.'

'So how was your trip to visit Maurice?' I asked.

'We had a great time, thanks for asking. Of course, he was on stage both nights, but we were still able to spend quite a bit of time together. We had planned to see the sights of Chester, maybe do some shopping, but we ended up spending most of the time in bed ...'

'That's far more information than we need,' Bayo said with a grin, 'but thanks for sharing anyway.'

'Isn't it hard, being in a long-distance relationship like that?' Even as I asked, I found myself thinking that if there'd been some distance in the relationship I'd had with Gavin, I might have had the opportunity to find out what he was really like much sooner.

'To be honest, since we got together, this is the first

128

time Maurice has had a role that's taken him out on the road for any length of time. Before that, he did eighteen months in the cast of *We Will Rock You*. I'm hoping that when this tour finishes, he'll get another job in the West End.' He ate a chip, then said, 'But we must be doing something right, because ...' He paused, as if wondering whether he ought to continue.

'Go on,' Bayo prompted.

'Well, I've been waiting for the right moment to tell you both, and now seems like as good a time as any. Maurice proposed to me last night, and I said yes. We're getting married at Christmas.'

'Oh, that's fantastic news.' I reached across the table and squeezed Dean's hand. 'Congratulations.'

'Yeah, well done, mate.' Bayo enveloped his friend in an awkward, blokey hug, and the delight on his face was genuine.

'So that's my news,' Dean said. 'What I'm more interested in is how you've been getting on with Gaynor in my absence, Bayo. Sure you don't have anything you need to let me know?'

'Oh, come on ...' A slight flush stained Bayo's cheeks. 'There is nothing going on between me and Gaynor Rhys.'

'So what about the care package she gave you, then?' Dean persisted.

'Care package?' Despite myself, I was intrigued.

'It's nothing. Gaynor had been doing some baking, and she brought a batch of Welsh cakes up to the apartment, that's all. They were for both of us, not just me.'

'Yeah, of course they were.' Dean scoffed. 'You're a lucky man, Bayo. When I was single, I never had men turning up on my doorstep bringing me homemade cake.'

'Look, it's not that I don't appreciate the gesture. Gaynor's a lovely woman. I'm just not interested in her in that way. Plus, even if I was, I'm going to be back in London in a couple of weeks. If I did get involved with her, I'd just feel like I was stringing her along.'

'What about you?' Dean turned his attention on me.

'What about me?' I crumpled up the grease-stained chip wrapper.

'Is there someone special in your life? We haven't really asked you.'

I shook my head, knowing I had to choose my words carefully so as not to give any indication that something might be going on between Rhodri and me. 'No, there's no one waiting for me back in London. I was engaged once, but … it didn't work out.' Aware that simple explanation wasn't going to satisfy the gossip-hungry Dean, I went on. 'He was a charming, funny guy; he'd been to the right school, the right university. All my friends thought we made a great couple.' I sighed as all the bad memories were dredged up. 'And then I found out what he was really like, how he'd got himself so far in debt he'd declared himself bankrupt to write it all off. He didn't want me for me, but for what being married to me could do for him. He was always talking about putting all our bank accounts in joint names, pooling our assets, looking into these dodgy little schemes that would help him shelter money from the taxman …'

'Sounds like he'd have been ideal for that documentary about male gold diggers we were working on,' Bayo commented idly.

Gold digger. Yes, that summed Gavin up nicely, even if it wasn't half as colourful as most of the things Kay had called him. 'You know, I think the best sex we ever had was the night he found out my dad was lining him up for a place on the company board. If I hadn't called off the wedding, he'd be burning his way through my money the way he burned through his own, making business decisions that could ruin the company, and I wouldn't be able to do a damn thing to stop him. So you can see why I'm not exactly rushing to go down that path again ...' I paused, recalling how excited Dean had been when he'd talked about accepting Maurice's proposal. 'But maybe I'm just a little cynical when it comes to marriage. And it could have been a lot worse. Gavin could have been hitting me, or seeing someone else behind my back.'

Bayo gathered up the litter of our meals, and tossed it into a nearby bin. He pulled a packet of cigarettes from his jacket pocket. 'I'm going to have one of these before we go back, if no one objects.'

'Fine by me,' I told him. Even though I didn't smoke, I didn't have a problem with people lighting up around me, as long as they were considerate.

He shook a couple of cigarette out of the packet, and offered one to Dean, who accepted. Then he produced a green plastic lighter, and lit each one in turn.

Bayo let out a plume of smoke from between his lips, and watched it curl up into the sky. 'You know, you shouldn't let an arsehole like that fiancé of yours ruin your opinion of men. We're not all cheats, or wife-beaters.'

'Or gold diggers,' Dean chipped in.

'I know that,' I assured them, having never intended to make a blanket condemnation of the entire male species. 'But since Dad died, all I've been concentrating on is making sure the company is run properly. Anthony Hotels has a great reputation, and I want to uphold that.'

Dean reached under the table, and brought his camera out from where he'd stowed it. 'You don't fancy saying all that again for the benefit of this thing, do you? The bit about making a success of the company, I mean, not all the stuff about that Gavin bloke. Although I'm sure Hugo would love some juicy scandal for the show.'

'There's not much point,' Bayo pointed out. 'Not when I didn't bring any of the sound equipment with me.'

'Anyway,' I said, spotting an opportunity to turn the conversation away from myself, 'if you'd wanted juicy scandal, you should have been in the hotel last night.'

Dean sat up a little straighter on the bench, his interest clearly piqued. 'Really? Do tell, babe.'

'I had to go and investigate a disturbance in one of the rooms on the third floor. You won't believe this, but I walked in on a couple playing a kinky sex game.'

'Seriously?' Bayo's eyes widened.

'Oh yes. She'd got him fastened to the bed and was beating him with a big rubber paddle.' I ran a hand through my hair, still not quite able to believe I'd witnessed such an extraordinary scene. 'And the best part of it was they'd booked into the hotel as Mr and Mrs Smith.'

'You're kidding.' Dean laughed. 'I thought that was just an urban myth. Although I did know a couple who used to play this game where they'd go into a hotel bar separately, and then one would chat the other up, like they were strangers to each other. Then they'd check into a room and spend all night fucking each other's brains out. Said it really added some spice to their relationship.'

'I mean, I'm not so naïve that I'm unaware this kind of

thing goes on,' I continued. 'In London particularly, lots of escort girls book rooms so they can entertain their clients there, however hard we try to prevent that kind of thing. But I just didn't expect it in a place like this …' I swept out my arm, indicating the stretch of sea front on which we sat.

'Maybe that's the documentary Hugo should be making,' Bayo commented. 'Hotel staff reveal what really goes on behind closed doors.'

'We should pitch the idea,' Dean said. 'What do they call those places in the States, the hotels where they turn a blind eye to people renting rooms just for a quickie?' He thought for a moment. 'No-tell motels, that's it. I'm sure we could persuade Hugo to go for it, send us off to Vegas or somewhere to film. Get Jane – sorry, Claudia – on board as a consultant …'

'Spending that time with Maurice has really perked you up, hasn't it?' Bayo said. 'I can't remember when I last saw you so full of enthusiasm about anything.'

'Well, when you spend four hours on a coach back from Chester, it does give you a lot of time to think about things, and all I know is I want my next assignment to involve filming somewhere a little more glamorous than here.' Dean stubbed out his cigarette. 'Come on, let's go back to the apartment and I'll put the kettle on. We're back on early starts tomorrow, and I need to make sure I've got everything ready.'

I followed the two men to where we'd parked the car, still thinking back to Bayo's remarks when I'd been talking about Gavin. He was right: there were plenty of decent men in the world, and I was sure I'd found one in Rhodri. But ours was a passing thing, a relationship that had no foundation in the real world, and I had to keep reminding myself of that.

TEN

Returning to the morning shift felt like coming home. For the first time in a week, I took my regular jog along the prom, though I couldn't help looking at the familiar stretch of hotels and shop fronts with new eyes. Ever since I'd read the file of correspondence between Alastair Hammond and my father, I'd been wondering what the influx of European money would mean to Aberpentre. I'd hoped to have a word with Rhodri, making out that I'd read an article in one of the newspapers about the regeneration grant and asking him if he knew anything about it. Would there be jobs for the local townsfolk, or just for the highly skilled software professionals Hammond saw as the potential buyers of his apartments? And what would happen to all the people who worked here if the hotel was sold? Now I was coming to know them as more than just names in a Human Resources file, I couldn't help feeling guilty about the prospect of putting them all out of work.

I was still mulling over those questions when a man I recognised strolled into the lobby towards the end of my shift. Before I could greet him, he said, 'Afternoon, I'm here to see Rhodri Wynn-Jones. We've got a meeting scheduled at – hang on, Claudia, what are you doing here?'

This was the moment I'd been dreading since I arrived at the hotel. Someone had seen through my disguise. I did the only thing I could in the circumstances, fixing him with a sweet smile and feigning ignorance. 'I'm sorry, sir, I think you must have mistaken me for someone else.'

'Oh come on, you know me. Pete Ashton, from the marketing team. I was only in your office a few weeks ago.' He looked at me, then at the camera, as if wondering whether I was trying to play some trick on him. 'Your hair looks great, by the way.'

I glared over at Dean, trying to convey with my expression that if he continued filming, I would walk over to him, rip off the arm that held the camera and beat him to death with the soggy end, but he remained oblivious. This was too good a moment for him to miss.

I lowered my voice, compelling Pete to lean a little closer. 'Pete, can I have a quiet word with you?'

'Sure.'

'Away from the camera would be best.' Getting out of my chair, I beckoned him to follow me round to the little corridor at the side of Reception. He leant against the lockers there, regarding me expectantly.

'Pete, this is a bit of a tricky situation, and I need your cooperation. Nobody here knows me as Claudia. I'm working undercover, filming for a TV show.'

'Oh … right. I've not just landed you in the shit or anything, have I?'

I shook my head. Behind Pete, I was aware of Dean, his lens now trained on us both. Though I'd hoped he might let us have this discussion in private, I knew he'd get a

136

chewing-out by Hugo and his team if he didn't have footage of the incident to send to them. 'It should be OK, but you may find yourself appearing in the show now.'

He shrugged. 'I think I can cope with my five minutes of fame. But your secret will be safe with me, I promise.'

'Thank you. Now come on, I need to let Rhodri know you're here. And don't be surprised if you hear him refer to me as Jane. That's the name I'm going by while I'm in Aberpentre.'

As Pete walked back into Reception with me, he said, 'So I suppose this disguise thing explains the hair and the glasses. That look really suits you, by the way.'

'Thanks, but I've got no intention of making it a permanent change.' I dialled Rhodri's extension and waited for him to answer. 'Hi, Rhodri, I have Pete Ashton from the Anthony Hotels marketing team here. He has an appointment with you.'

'Thanks, Jane. Send him through.'

I smiled at Pete. 'He's ready for you. His office is down the hall, second door on the right.'

When he'd ambled off to meet Rhodri, I turned to Dean and Bayo. 'You two got every last word of that, didn't you?'

Dean nodded. 'Sorry, but we had to. I'm sure you understand why.' He gave me a beseeching look. 'You wouldn't mind giving your opinion to camera, would you, babe? Just so we can get your reaction to someone recognising you like that.'

There was only one answer I could give. 'Of course.'

He raised the camera, and asked, 'So how do you know this Pete guy, anyway?'

'I know Pete because he's been part of our marketing

and sales department for about three years now. And he was in a meeting with me recently because we're thinking of adding some new products to the complimentary items we offer to our guests. We'd agreed to have some samples made up and trialled in a random selection of the company's hotels. And this was one of the hotels we'd chosen.' A fact I'd completely forgotten till Pete wandered into the lobby, though I decided against sharing that piece of information with Dean. 'Being out of the office for the last couple of weeks, I hadn't realised those items were ready to go.'

'And how did you feel when Pete recognised you?'

'When he called me Claudia, I was just hoping that no one from the hotel staff was in earshot. I don't know how long I could have kept telling him that he didn't know me when he obviously does. But I think the crisis has been averted for the time being.'

Dean stopped filming. 'That's great. I'll let you get back to work now.'

Ten minutes later, Pete came back into Reception. This time, he had Rhodri with him. The two men stopped in front of the desk and shook hands.

'Thanks so much for that, Pete,' Rhodri said. 'We'll make sure they go in all the rooms. And I'll be in touch as soon as we start getting comments from guests.'

'That'll be great. If you could just make sure the new feedback forms are handed out at the end of each stay, instead of the ones you've been using up till now. Once the trial period's over, you can go back to the old forms.'

'Not a problem,' Rhodri assured him. 'I'll let Jane and the rest of the receptionists know about the change.'

As Pete walked away, he turned his head and gave me a

little wink, as if to let me know that he hadn't spilled my secret. But I didn't relax fully until he'd left the building.

Before Rhodri could think about returning to his office, I said, 'So, you're going to let me know about what, exactly?'

'Oh, we've been asked to leave some new items in the rooms for our guests to use and take away. And we've been given updated forms so we can specifically get their comments on whether they've found these items have improved the quality of their stay.'

'Sounds interesting. Am I allowed to ask what these mysterious new goodies are?'

'You can do better than that. You can let me show you. Back in a minute ...'

Rhodri disappeared down the corridor, heading for his office. In his absence, I busied myself removing the current feedback forms from their folder in the filing cabinet. The company's standard procedure involved giving one to guests when they checked out. If they didn't have time to fill in the form before they left, they could go online and complete a short satisfaction survey on the Anthony Hotels website. I vaguely remembered our IT experts saying they'd be able to adapt the form so guests staying at the hotels where these new items were being tested out could offer their thoughts, but at the time, I hadn't thought too deeply about the practicalities of the scheme. I'd certainly never expected to find myself working on the front desk of a hotel that had been chosen for the trial.

When Rhodri returned, he had a sheaf of white, thin card forms in one hand, and a small, transparent plastic bag in the other, of the kind used to hold the napkin and cutlery sets that accompany airline meals. He set the cards on the counter, and gave the top one to me.

'Here are the new questions –' Rhodri picked up a ballpoint pen and tapped at the relevant line on the form.

'Did you use the "good night's sleep pack"?' I read aloud. 'If so, how would you rate it out of five?'

Beneath those questions were a couple of lines where guests could leave any further comments they might have.

'So what's in this pack, then?' I asked, even though I already knew the answer.

Rhodri tore open the plastic bag, and withdrew an eye mask, which he gave to me. I'd seen the prototype during a meeting, but now I held the finished version. Made of nylon and backed with soft jersey fabric, it bore a discreet Anthony Hotels logo on the front.

'Apparently,' Rhodri said, 'one of the most common complaints we receive across the whole chain concerns the quality of sleep our guests get. Of course, a lot of factors can affect that – how firm the mattress is, the temperature of the room, how much someone's had to drink before they go to bed … But some people find it hard to sleep because of the amount of light coming into the room. The blackout curtains we have in all the rooms are designed to help with that.'

'Unless you've got a room that overlooks the promenade at Blackpool when the Illuminations are lit,' I suggested.

'Perhaps not, in which case someone at head office thought these masks would be a nice touch. And of course, all the curtains in the world can't do anything if it's noise that's keeping someone awake. So the sleep packs also contain these …'

Rhodri opened a small box, and shook a pair of yellow foam rubber earplugs into his palm. I wondered if they'd have done anything to prevent the disturbance I'd had to deal with in Room 304, or whether Mr Smith's cries of pain and pleasure would have been audible even with them in.

'We're going to be putting one of these packs in each room, but you'll also be expected to keep some here in Reception, in case any of the guests ask for them.'

'Seems like a good idea.' I gave the eye mask back to him.

'Well, we'll only know that once the comments start coming in. But if the reaction is generally positive, then the plan is that they will become a permanent feature in all the hotels.' Rhodri leant close in to me, and murmured, 'You know, Jane, I was thinking we could help the company with their research on this, provide some feedback of our own.'

The low, husky timbre to his voice sent a shiver of pleasure through me. 'And how would we do that, exactly?'

'Well … Hey, Tom. Is it that time already?'

I looked up to see the young receptionist striding into the lobby, his hands in his pockets and big, metallic red headphones jammed over his ears. Glancing at the clock on the wall, I realised it was almost four o'clock, and the end of my shift.

'Rhodri, Jane, how's it going?' Tom pulled the headphones down so they were resting around his neck. I caught the tinny blast of rap music in the moments before he brought his MP3 player out from his pocket and switched it off.

'Fine,' Rhodri replied, 'and that's really good timing on your part.'

Is it? I wanted to ask, sure that Rhodri had been about to whisper some naughty little fantasy in my ear when Tom walked in.

'And why's that?'

'I've just been explaining to Jane about these "good night's sleep" kits we're going to be putting in all the rooms.' Rhodri quickly talked Tom through the reasoning behind the pack, and the new forms that accompanied their use, while I collected my things together and prepared to go home.

A moment later, I walked into the lobby, my bag slung over my shoulder. 'Well, goodnight, Rhodri, Tom ...'

'Oh, Jane,' Rhodri said. I turned to see him stuffing something into his jacket pocket. 'Would you mind coming through to my office before you go? I need to discuss something with you.'

'Sure.' Wondering what he needed to speak to me about that couldn't wait till I was back at work tomorrow I followed Rhodri down the hall.

Once inside the office, he locked the door, turning to me with a wolfish grin. 'There. That should make sure we're not disturbed. Now, about that research I wanted you to help me with ...' He brought the eye mask from his pocket. It dangled suggestively from one finger.

'Of course. Just let me know what you need me to do.'

'Put this on.' It sounded more like an instruction than a request.

I did as he asked, taking off my glasses and putting them on his desk. Once the mask was on, I adjusted it till it sat comfortably over my eyes.

'How does that feel, Jane?'

'Not too bad.' In truth, standing in the middle of his office, blindfolded, was a little disorientating. Not a sliver of light crept under the edge of the soft fabric, and I could only make out Rhodri's position by the gentle sound of his breathing close by. My other senses seemed to be heightened, compensating for my lack of sight, and I almost jumped when I heard his voice again.

'So you can't see what I'm doing?'

'No …'

'Well, this should prove whether you're telling the truth.' With that, he put his arms round me from behind, and began to unfasten my jacket.

'Rhodri, what are you doing?' It was barely a protest. I'd guessed that he planned to seduce me; I just hadn't worked out until now how the eye mask would be involved.

'Remember what I said to you, about you coming on my command?' As he spoke, he pulled the jacket down off my arms. I heard him throw it aside, but had no idea where it landed. 'Well, I didn't have any idea of how I was going to make that happen, until that Pete guy arrived with this little beauty.' He ran a finger under the elasticated strap of the eye mask, close to my ear. The movement turned into a subtle caress, as he stroked the backs of his fingers down the side of my neck. His hand came to rest at the neckline of my blouse.

'You want this, don't you?'

'Yes.' The word was little more than a whisper, as my body shuddered with the prospect of the pleasure to come. When I'd burst in on poor Mr Smith, I'd wondered what it might be like to find myself in a similar position,

143

blindfolded and at the mercy of my lover's whims. Now, it seemed I was about to find out.

'I want you to relax,' Rhodri said, beginning to undo the buttons on my blouse. 'But remember, there's only one rule to this game. You're not allowed to come until I say so.'

How hard could that be, I wondered. Then Rhodri brushed his hand over my breasts, now clad in only a thin microfibre bra, and I felt a little, rippling thrill low down in my belly. His touch seemed magnified, all my senses focused on the progress of his fingers, moving in a slow, spiralling trail down my stomach.

The blouse was off now; tossed to join my jacket, I assumed. Somehow, not being able to see what was happening as Rhodri systematically stripped me made it all the more exciting.

'You have such a gorgeous body, Jane.' Rhodri's tone was hypnotic, and I relaxed against him as he brought his hands back up to my chest. 'Such lovely tits. Just the right size to fit in my palms, with nothing wasted ...' His actions mimicked his words, and again his thumbs strummed across my aching nipples.

A little whimper escaped from my lips. Could you come just from having your breasts played with? I'd never contemplated the idea before, but as Rhodri continued to stroke and tease the hard little nubs that strained towards his fingers, it seemed all too possible. Between my legs, I was liquid, swollen, a pulse beating fiercely there.

Lulled by Rhodri's caresses, I didn't resist as he undid the catch of my bra. I was enjoying this far too much to think about asking him to slow down, to give me a moment to get over the sweet shock of exposure as he bared my breasts. He whipped the bra off with a flourish, as though presenting me to some unknown audience.

I knew he'd stepped away from me, because I no longer felt the warm, solid pressure of his body against my back. Stupidly, I turned my head from side to side, trying to see where he'd gone even though the eye mask was designed to prevent me from doing just that.

'Rhodri?' The word was little more than a squeak. We were alone; he'd made sure no one could walk in on us. Yet I still couldn't help feeling vulnerable, my world thrown totally off balance by being made to stand topless in my boss's office.

'It's OK, sweetheart, I'm here.' His voice came from somewhere in front of me. I heard the squeak of metal, and realised he must have taken a seat in the swivel chair that stood before his desk. 'Put your hands on your head for me. I want to take a good, long look at you ...'

I did as he asked, aware that the movement would lift my breasts and thrust them out towards him. He gave a soft grunt, registering his approval.

'Good girl,' he said at length. 'Now, I want you to walk over to me, and bend over my lap.' As I took a stumbling step forward, he added, 'It's OK, you can drop your hands now.'

Slowly, I approached him, guided by the scent of his woody aftershave and the steady rise and fall of his breathing. It was so quiet in the room that even the ticking of the watch on Rhodri's wrist was audible.

After no more than four paces, I bumped up against Rhodri's knees, and let out a surprised, "Ooh!"

In response, he gave a soft chuckle, clearly amused by the bizarre predicament in which he'd placed me. 'Come on, now, over my knee.'

I was reminded of something he'd said when we'd been talking dirty to each other on the phone. *I'd drag you over my knee and give you a good spanking …* At the time, the thought had excited me, but if that was the track Rhodri's mind now ran along, I wasn't sure I was ready for the reality.

As if picking up on my hesitation, 'Don't worry, Jane, I won't make you do anything you really don't want to. You can call a halt to this any time you want.'

'No, it's OK,' I said, as much to reassure myself as him. 'I can do this. It's just a little odd, not being able to see, that's all.'

'Just think of this as product research, sweetheart. When these masks go into the guest rooms, you'll have the satisfaction of knowing they do the job properly.'

As he spoke, he took my arm, and guided me onto his lap, face down. Lying there wasn't so bad, I was pleasantly relieved to discover. His thighs were spread wide to support my weight, though I couldn't help but be aware of the hard bulge at his crotch. The game was clearly getting to him, and he was probably getting an extra jolt of excitement from being in charge.

He smoothed a hand over my skirt-covered bum cheeks, working in slow, soothing circles. The motion relaxed me; it began to feel strangely right to be draped across his knees, half-dressed and waiting to have my bottom smacked.

'Do you want to know why I'm going to spank you?' he enquired.

'Because you can?' I retorted.

He sighed. 'No, it's because of exactly that attitude. I'm

146

not prepared to put up with any more of your sassiness, your attempts to take charge. You need to remember just who the boss is around here.'

Oh, I knew that. When it came to the chain of command at Anthony Hotels, Rhodri Wynn-Jones was way beneath me in the pecking order. I was the big boss, the woman who made all the decisions that would shape his future, and that of his staff. At least, that was the situation in the real world. At this moment, the man was very much in control, and try as I might to deny it, I liked the way the roles had been temporarily reversed.

'So now we've reminded ourselves of who's in charge ...' Without giving me any more time to prepare, Rhodri brought his hand down on my backside. The blow wasn't hard, and the fabric of my skirt muffled its impact, but still I squirmed on his lap.

'Stay still, Jane, or I might have to raise your skirt.'

The thought of Rhodri carrying out his threat, pushing up the tight black polyester till my bottom was revealed to him in the thin, nude-coloured panties that matched my long-since-discarded bra, only had me wriggling harder. His strong hand in the small of my back kept me in place.

'You're such a bad girl to disobey me. I really hoped you'd learnt your lesson, but it seems I still need to teach you how to behave ...' Rhodri punctuated his words with a short series of swats, aiming them at each of my cheeks in turn. Then he did as he'd promised, and turned his attention to my skirt. The rasping sound as the zip came down seemed awfully loud in the small office. Though I made a half-hearted attempt to stop him, kicking my legs to try and make the task more difficult, he pulled the garment off.

I couldn't have dreamed when he invited me into his office that I'd find myself in this position, lying in Rhodri's lap wearing nothing but a pair of panties that didn't really cover much of anything.

'You look adorable,' he said. 'It almost makes me think twice about doing this.' He smacked me again, and again. Six sharp slaps that sent little bursts of pain sizzling through my flesh. But as the pain faded, it left in its wake a dark, blossoming pleasure, melding and mingling till the two sensations became one. And between each blow, he rubbed at my bottom, soothing away the ache he'd created and making me delirious for more.

Rhodri must have noticed the change in my reactions. Where I'd fought at first to move away from his palm, now I pressed my rump back at it, almost welcoming the punishment. Which is precisely when he stopped.

'Oh Jane, you took that so well. But you do remember the point of this whole exercise, don't you?'

I could have expressed ignorance, or made some smart remark designed to earn me another few spanks, but I was beyond that. Rhodri had stoked the fire within me, and now I needed him to quench it before it burned out of control.

'You want me to come, but not till you give your permission.'

'That's right. Maybe I underestimated you. Perhaps you are a quick learner, after all …'

He stroked a finger over my panties, right at the spot where they were soaked with my juices. Almost absentmindedly, he repeated the movement, caressing me through the wet material.

'Please, Rhodri,' I begged, not sure whether I was

asking him to stop or carry on. He must know the effect his touch had on me. I wished I could see his face, and watch the play of emotions upon it. Even though it would take very little of this treatment to have me soaring to the summit of pleasure, I had to try and hold on to my self-control till Rhodri allowed me to come.

When he slipped a finger under the crotch of my underwear, I let out a gasp. The feeling of his calloused fingertip rubbing against my clit, with nothing to shield me from his touch, was too much.

'Can't – can't hold back,' I muttered. 'Please … I need to come.'

'What would you do if I told you to get up, put your clothes on, and leave the office?' He chuckled to himself. 'Maybe I should do that. Send you home right now. After all, we've proved the eye masks do their job.'

He wouldn't be so cruel, surely. I said nothing, holding my breath in fear that he might withdraw his touch, leaving me unsatisfied.

'But you've been a good girl, Jane. You've done everything I asked of you. And so I'm going to give you what you want.' He returned to stroking my nub; feather-light flicks of his finger that had me gasping and writhing against the coarse weave of his trousers. 'That's it,' he urged. 'Come for me.'

The longed-for command pushed me over the edge. If he hadn't been holding me steady, I might well have fallen off his lap. A starburst of colours, neon bright, danced behind my eyelids, and I sobbed out in bliss.

When Rhodri spoke, his voice seemed to come from a very long way away.

'Hey, that's it, you're fine now …' He guided me up

149

until I sat on his knees, and we shared a long, lingering kiss. At last, he removed the eye mask. I blinked against the sudden brightness.

A bottle of water stood on Rhodri's desk. He reached over and picked it up as I clung to him. When he'd unscrewed the cap, he put the mouth of the bottle to my lips and I drank thirstily.

'Thank you,' I said. 'That was ... intense. I never expected being blindfolded to make such a difference.' Rhodri's cock still poked up at me behind his fly. 'But I think we still need to do something about this.' I grazed my fingertips over the hard bulge. 'I mean, I've had my pleasure. It seems only fair that you get yours.'

I got down from his lap, settling myself on the floor between his widely parted thighs. Rhodri didn't object as I tugged open his belt buckle, then unzipped his trousers.

'Maybe you should be wearing the eye mask?' I suggested, as I reached in to take hold of his shaft. 'See if it does anything to heighten your experience.'

He shook his head, but I could see from the flash of excitement in his eyes that he had not dismissed the idea out of hand. What a thrill it would be to have him bound to the chair with his own belt, blindfolded and helpless, but that could wait till another time. Right now, I was content just to stroke my hand along that rigid length from base to tip, easing the soft sleeve of skin down and away from its domed head.

'Such a big, beautiful thing, and all mine to enjoy,' I crooned, then bent my head close and took it between my lips. Rhodri's breath caught in his throat as I swallowed more of him down, relishing his salty maleness, and the silky liquid that seeped from his tip. When I looked up, his eyes were half-closed and he seemed lost in his own world, transported by the little licks and flickers of my tongue over his flesh.

I let him slip from my lips long enough to say, 'You like that, don't you?'

He could only nod, and I knew I had Rhodri just where I wanted him. This time, when I plunged my head back down, I took as much of him as I could. Now, the movements of my head were faster, more frantic, and I shuttled my fist up and down the portion of his cock I had not been able to fit in my mouth.

He was just about able to spit out words of warning, alerting me to his imminent eruption, and then my mouth was suddenly full. I swallowed, wiped my mouth with the back of my hand, and rose a little awkwardly to my feet. Rhodri gazed down at me with a blissed-out smirk.

'If I ever get to meet whoever recommended they try out the "good night's sleep" packs in this hotel, I'm going to shake their hand.'

I paused in the act of retrieving my bra from where it hung on the corner of a filing cabinet. Rhodri was closer to the person who had given the go-ahead for the trial than he would ever know. It was just one of the increasing number of secrets I found myself keeping from him.

'So if you were to fill in a feedback form …?'

He grinned. The look on his face told me he wasn't thinking about the eye mask. 'Five stars, all the way.'

152

ELEVEN

Rhodri caught up with me as I left the hotel on Thursday evening, running down the hotel steps and calling my name. For a moment, I thought I might have dropped something in the lobby, but he said, 'Jane, I need to ask another favour of you. You don't have to say yes if you've got other plans, but can you do a couple of hours' overtime on Saturday?'

What other plans did he think I might have, exactly? Going shopping for clothes with Dean? Joining Bayo for a round of eighteen holes at Criccieth golf course? Even though I couldn't help wondering if there might be a catch, I said, 'Of course.'

'Great. I should have mentioned it earlier, but we've got a wedding reception in the function room.'

'Really?' I thought of the Anthony in Leeds, which had been booked up for weddings almost a year in advance. 'Is that a regular thing here?'

He shook his head. 'It used to be, up until a couple of years ago. With all the changes in management, that side of the business kind of fell by the wayside. But it's such a good source of income we've been stupid to ignore it. So, three or four months ago I got posters put up in the local dress hire shops and parish noticeboards, advertising the venue as being available once more. This is the first booking we've had as a result of that.'

Without being aware of it, he'd just added to the list of reasons I was compiling on why we should keep the hotel as a going concern.

'The first of many, I hope?' I asked with a smile.

'Well, we've certainly had a few enquiries, mostly for later in the year. To be honest, I hadn't really expected anyone to want to use the room so soon, when you think how long in advance most people tend to make the arrangements for their weddings. But it seems this couple got let down by some country house hotel just outside Llanbedrog, who'd double-booked them, so we stepped in and provided an alternative venue.'

'So what would you need me to do?'

'Well, I'm having trouble rounding up as many waiting staff as I'm going to need. I spoke to the temp agency we use, but most of the people on their books are already otherwise engaged on Saturday. So –' at least he had the grace to look sheepish, '– I wondered if you'd be prepared to help out.'

'Would this be silver service? Because that's something I've had no experience of.' Unlike when I'd told Rhodri I didn't know how to clean rooms, I wasn't lying. In all my years learning about every aspect of running a hotel, I had never worked in a dining room.

'Jane, I've got every faith in you. Whatever I've asked you to do so far, you haven't let me down. I'm sure this will be just the same.'

His words reassured me, but only a little. 'OK.'

'The wedding's at 2.30, and the guests should be

arriving here just after four. That'll give you time to get changed after your shift, though all you'll really have to do is lose the jacket and put on a black waistcoat. If you don't have one of those, don't rush out and buy one. We keep a couple of spares on hand in case of spillages, and there should be one in your size.' He thought for a moment, as if wondering whether he'd forgotten to mention anything. 'I think that's probably all you need to know.'

'Oh, one thing,' I said, as a thought occurred to me. 'If you're asking me to step outside my comfort zone, then I'm going to have the camera crew following me, just in case anything goes horribly wrong. You might want to check with the happy couple, make sure they're OK with Dean filming their reception.'

'Leave that with me. And Jane ... Thanks so much for helping me out with this. I'm losing count of all the ways I'm so grateful to you.'

He put his arms around me, and I relaxed into the hug. We hadn't spent any real time together since he'd spanked me in his office, and my body seemed to awaken at his touch, needing more.

Across the road, I thought I saw a familiar cloud of blonde curls, and I forced myself to pull away from Rhodri. If that was Angharad Williams, I didn't want her to see us together. I didn't need to give the woman any more reasons to dislike me.

'I'll see you tomorrow,' I said.

'Before you go –' He caught hold of my hand, briefly linking his fingers with my own. 'If you're not doing anything tomorrow night, would you like to go out somewhere?'

I thought back to the previous Friday, and how much I'd enjoyed having dinner with Rhodri. 'I'd love to.'

'Great.'

Was it my imagination, or was Rhodri blushing slightly? After all the deliciously naughty things we'd done together, was he actually shy when it came to asking me on a date? He couldn't honestly think I might turn him down.

I dropped a gentle kiss on his cheek, no longer caring who might be watching us, and wished him goodnight.

Rather than going straight back to Bay Vista, I headed for the convenience store a couple of streets away, in search of milk, bread, and breakfast cereal. Trying to make a choice between crunchy nut cornflakes or granola with honey and almonds, I was startled by a voice in my ear.

'I know what you're doing here.'

When I turned round, I found Angharad glaring at me. Just what I needed: the close personal attention of Rhodri's borderline stalker of an ex-girlfriend.

'Hi Angharad, lovely to see you. How did the quiz night go?' I reached for the nearest packet of cereal, anxious to avoid any possible confrontation.

'I saw you with Rhodri just now, all over him like a rash.'

'Not that it's any of your business –' I kept my voice low, not wanting to attract the attention of any nearby shoppers, '– but I'd just agreed to do some overtime for Rhodri and he was thanking me for getting him out of a hole.'

'Yeah, and I can think of a few holes you'd like him to get into. You might act the innocent, but I know who you really are, Jane Ennis.'

She almost spat the name at me, and I tried not to flinch. She couldn't possibly have discovered my real identity, could she? Her next words proved that my fears were unfounded.

'You think that if you let him get into your knickers, then he'll give you a job in the hotel. It's written all over your face.'

I almost wanted to laugh out loud. It was a good job Angharad worked in a wine bar, because she would have made a terrible psychologist.

'Well, if that's what you want to believe ... Now if you'll excuse me, I need to pay for my shopping.'

Brushing past her, I strode down the aisle to the self-service till. She could think what she wanted about my motives for spending time with Rhodri. I wasn't going to let the woman get to me any longer.

When I left the shop, my purchases in a carrier bag, I looked back to see if I was still being watched, but Angharad had gone.

Back in the apartment, I made myself a cup of strong tea, and took it through to the living room. The blanks Dad's training had left in my waitressing knowledge could be filled in by the internet, or so I hoped. Opening my browser, I typed "silver service waiting tips" into the search field and was gratified by the number of resulting hits. By the time I'd finished reading through a couple of the most promising articles, I'd acquired a decent grasp of the basics. Food and drinks were served from the guest's right-hand side, and removed from the same side. Meals had to be transferred from serving platters to the diner's plate using a fork and spoon: a manoeuvre that filled me with dread as I considered how easy it would be to drop items into the lap of an unsuspecting diner. Even the placing of the various foodstuffs had to follow a set pattern: meat at the front of the plate, potatoes on top, and vegetables to the side, though I couldn't help wondering whether the guests would notice if I got that wrong. As for pouring wine, that appeared to be an art in itself, and I made a mental note to make sure that I had a corkscrew with me on Saturday; somehow, I couldn't see us serving wedding guests with anything that came from a screw-top bottle.

Maybe I could persuade one of the senior waiters at the Anthony to give me a crash course, just as Wioletta had detailed everything I needed to do in order to clean a room to her standards. If nothing else, it would provide Dean with some interesting footage for *Secret CEO*.

Thinking of my tame cameraman made me realise I hadn't yet alerted him and Bayo to the news that I would be working overtime on Saturday. I reached for my phone, and called Dean's number.

'Hey, babe, to what do I owe the pleasure?' he said by way of greeting.

'Hi, Dean, I hope you didn't have any plans for Saturday evening.'

'Oh, nothing that didn't involve vegging out in front of *American Idol* and stuffing my face with pizza. Why?'

'Well, I'm afraid you're going to have to watch it on catch-up.' Quickly, I outlined what Rhodri had requested of me. 'I could have said no, but that wouldn't have been fair on him, not when he's short of staff. And anyway, I was thinking of the look on Hugo Murray's face when you tell him you've got footage of me working as a silver service waitress at a wedding reception.'

'You're all heart. Rhodri does know we have to get all the guests to sign release forms, to say they're happy for us to show them on TV?'

'I've made him aware of that. Though I suppose you could take lots of arty close-ups of me spooning food onto plates, with no faces visible. No one could object to that, surely.'

'Leave it with me. And don't worry about Saturday. Hugo's been watching the footage I sent over of you working with the housekeeping team, and the incident with the lift, and reading between the lines, you're coming across great. He thinks you have great chemistry with Rhodri, by the way ...'

What was that supposed to mean? I wondered as I put the phone down. It hadn't taken me long to work out that what Hugo had been hoping for was a clash in personalities between Rhodri and me. There'd been so much potential, given that we came from such contrasting backgrounds and had such differing experiences of life. And, at first, Rhodri had clearly resented the manner in which I'd been parachuted in to work at the hotel. Maybe if we hadn't gone for dinner together, spent a little time getting to know each other, he would still feel the same way. But the attraction we had for each other would still have been there, bubbling beneath the surface like lava; apply enough in the way of pressure and it would have erupted.

I've never been one of those women who thrive on drama, who need to provoke an argument in order to get a reaction from the man they desire. If I'd found myself fighting with Rhodri, it would have been because he'd driven me to the point of distraction, just as I'd had some spectacularly messy rows with Gavin in the days before I'd told him to get out of my life for good. Hugo Murray could have got a six-part series out of those fights.

It was just as well, I supposed, that Hugo didn't know the truth of my relationship with my temporary boss. But as far as I knew, no one was aware of my secret trysts in Rhodri's office, and in the lift, and I would do my damnedest to keep it that way. I'd already laid enough of my private life on the line for this show; revealing any more could only end badly, I was sure.

TWELVE

I slipped out of Bay Vista apartments just before seven, hoping I wouldn't bump into Bayo or Dean as I left. They were off to see the latest *X-Men* film at Aberpentre's sole cinema, the Screenhouse, and they'd invited me to join them. I felt guilty about turning them down, telling them I planned on having a bubble bath and an early night. It would have been fun to spend the evening at the flicks, munching popcorn and cheering on Hugh Jackman and his cohorts. But it was a necessary lie. I didn't want the two men to get even the faintest idea that I'd actually lined up a date with the luscious Mr Wynn-Jones.

As before, Rhodri and I arranged to meet outside the hotel. This time I was the first to arrive, and I took a moment to pull out my mirrored compact and check my lipstick. Tonight, I wore an Aztec print maxidress, flat, gladiator-style sandals and a denim jacket. The halter neck of the dress made wearing a bra impractical, and when I'd been getting dressed, I'd debated leaving off my panties too, imagining Rhodri's reaction when he discovered what I'd done. But that seemed a step too far even for Jane.

Strange how playing this role had encouraged me to experiment with the wilder side of my sexuality, giving in to temptations I'd avoided till now. When I'd been with Gavin, I'd never dreamed of anything as kinky as letting him blindfold me. Maybe, deep down, I just hadn't trusted him the way I'd already come to trust Rhodri in such a short space of time.

'Good evening, gorgeous.' Rhodri, freshly shaven and looking relaxed in a long-sleeved khaki T-shirt and jeans, wandered up to me. 'Are you ready to hit the town?'

I hung back for a moment. 'Where did you have in mind? Only I bunked off a trip to the cinema with Bayo and Dean, and I'd hate to bump into them when they think I'm at home, washing my hair.' In truth, I half expected them to come walking towards us at any moment, heading to catch the 7.45 screening.

'In which case, I know the perfect place. Have you been down to the pier yet?'

I shook my head. Though I'd intended to explore more of the town, something connected to the filming of *Secret CEO* always seemed to eat into my free time.

'Then tonight's the perfect night for me to show you what makes this town special. Come on, let's go.'

Rhodri took my hand, and we strolled along the sea front. A light breeze whipped at the ends of my hair, and I caught the sound of a bassline, borne on the wind from some nearby bar. The early summer evening stretched out ahead of us, full of promise, and at that moment there was nowhere I would rather have been.

As we reached the pier head, Rhodri pointed out a cream-painted building on the corner of the street opposite. 'That's Bellini's, where Angharad works. Not that I'm suggesting we go inside or anything …'

'But it is the best wine bar in town.' I laughed. 'And I

162

wouldn't say no to a nice glass of rosé.' I bent close to his ear and spoke in a suggestive tone. 'But wouldn't it be more fun if we bought a bottle later, and drank it in bed?'

'Don't say that, Jane. I'm going to be spending all evening thinking of taking you home and getting you naked.'

'Good,' I replied with an impish grin. 'But why don't you show me the delights of Aberpentre pier first?'

We wandered along the weathered wooden boards, through the gaps in which the sea below was visible as it beat against the rocks. The pier itself was dotted with a collection of little shops, selling everything from buckets and spades to postcards with views of Aberpentre and the surrounding area to dolls in the traditional Welsh dress of long black skirt, red shawl, and tall stovepipe hat.

I pressed my nose up against the window of a shop that stocked all manner of practical jokes and novelties. 'Hey, look, stink bombs. I didn't know they still made those things.'

'And just what would you know about stink bombs?' Rhodri spun me around to face him, as if he intended to interrogate me about the secrets of my past.

'Oh, let's just say when I was at school they were a great way of getting out of maths lessons …' I didn't add that the school in question was one of the most exclusive all-girls' institutions in the country, from which I had twice come close to being expelled. Jane Ennis would have attended her local comprehensive, and been proud of it.

'Now this is my favourite.' Rhodri returned his attention to the display. 'The squirty flower, designed for a gentleman's lapel. Given that I have never known any man to sport a buttonhole outside of a wedding, surely the fact you're wearing one at all is a dead giveaway you're planning to soak someone with it.'

'You know what we should do?' I couldn't suppress the wicked thought that came to me. 'Buy some of those ice cubes with the fake flies in them, go into Angharad's wine bar, drop one in our drinks, and see if we can set the people from Environmental Health on to her.'

'Now that's mean, but I like the way you're thinking ...'

Rhodri dragged me away from the kiosk before I could start plotting any more evil schemes. At the end of the pier, we leant against the iron railing, topped with a thick wooden handrail, and I gazed out to sea.

'Looks beautiful out there tonight,' I commented. 'So still and peaceful ...'

'I like it out here on stormy days,' Rhodri admitted. 'When the rain's churning up the waves and you've pretty much got the whole place to yourself. Of course, I'm too young to remember the pier the way it used to be.'

'How do you mean, used to be?'

'This is the second longest pier in Wales, after the one at Llandudno. When it was first built back in the 1870s, it had a theatre on the end. All the big music hall names played there – Max Miller, Old Mother Riley, even Ernie Wise when he was just a kid, before he teamed up with Eric Morecambe ... But during the Second World War, when the Germans blitzed this part of the coast, a stray bomb hit the theatre; pretty much destroyed it. When they eventually came to rebuild the pier, there wasn't the money to restore the theatre, so they just knocked it down.' He let go of his grip on the handrail, and turned back in the direction we'd come. 'Now, do you want to get some candyfloss, or do you want to play a game?'

'That depends what kind of game you have in mind.

'Come with me and I'll show you.'

We walked into the small arcade, which had a row of old-fashioned one-armed bandits, and one of those games I remembered from my childhood, where little rakes pushed down piles of two-penny pieces that teetered on the edge of a platform, convincing you it would only take a couple more coins to send the whole lot tumbling your way.

'I love these old things,' Rhodri said, 'but I never have any luck with them.' As if to demonstrate, he dropped a penny into the slot of the nearest fruit machine and pulled the handle. The display whirled and came to land, three lemons in a row. With a noisy clink, dozens of pennies came spilling out of the machine. He shrugged as he scooped up his winnings. 'OK, so maybe I do.'

Having walked over to the kiosk where the cashier sat, he exchanged the stack of pennies for ten-penny coins. 'Now let me show you what I'm really good at.'

'Oh, I already know about that, but surely you wouldn't be quite so naughty in public?'

'Behave yourself,' he warned me, but the twinkle in my eye told me he enjoyed the teasing as much as I did. 'This is what I had in mind.'

Rhodri led the way to a glass booth, filled partway with a variety of stuffed toys and other prizes. A three-pronged claw dangled from the ceiling, designed to scoop up the various prizes.

'Now, is there anything you particularly fancy?' he asked. 'A teddy? A gonk? The thing that could be the world's most evil-looking Chihuahua?'

'Surprise me. Those things are fixed, anyway. No one ever manages to grip anything long enough to win it.'

'Hey, I got three lemons, didn't I? I'm on a roll.' He fed the required amount of money into the machine, and pulled the joystick until the claw was directly in line with a white plush rabbit. Then he plunged it down, hooked the toy, and by some complicated manoeuvre, managed to drop it down the chute in the seconds before his time ran out and the claw went limp again. He fished in the tray, and brought out the little bunny, which he presented to me.

'See, told you I was good. I learned everything you need to know about these machines the summer I was seventeen, trying to win a teddy bear for Allison Evans …'

'Did you manage it?'

'Yeah, but by the time I did, Jason Lomas had passed his driving test and got the keys to his dad's Escort XR3i. Who do you think she was going to choose to go out with?'

'Well, I won't turn you down in favour of anyone who drives a flashy car – or even an Escort, for that matter.' I hugged the plush toy to myself, before popping it into my shoulder bag. 'And to say thank you for my lovely rabbit, I'll even treat you to that candy floss you were talking about.'

'OK, but before we do that, I want to show you something else. I promised you a tour of the sights, didn't I?'

We walked back to the pier head, and carried on for another fifty yards or so, until we came to what appeared to be a drinking fountain set into the sea wall. When it had first been installed, it must have been an impressive fixture, but now the stylised dolphins that surrounded the scallop-edged bowl into which water still ran were stained with verdigris. The lettering on a small plaque at the side of the fountain was disfigured by the same blue-green patina, making it almost impossible to read, though I thought I saw the words "Edward, Prince Regent" and part of a date.

'What is this?' I asked, running my hand over the tarnished metal.

'Aberpentre's a spa town, right? Like Bath and Cheltenham. Well, these are the famous waters. Rich in sulphur; very good for your health.'

'This is what everyone came here for?' Gazing at the slow, brackish-looking trickle, I found it hard to believe.

'Yeah, but like a lot of things, it just fell out of fashion. Go on, Jane, have a taste.'

'It's safe to drink?' I glanced at him, unconvinced.

'Absolutely. And to prove it, I'll go first.'

He cupped his hands beneath the waterspout, then raised them to his lips and drank. He grimaced, like a child who's just been made to take a spoonful of medicine, then looked expectantly at me.

Here went nothing. I copied Rhodri, letting the water splash into my hands. It had a strange aroma that reminded me of nothing more than Bonfire Night. When I drank, it tasted as disgusting as it smelled. 'Ugh, that's horrible!'

'Well, I'll admit it's an acquired taste …' He grinned. 'There was some talk about giving this fountain a facelift a few years back, but the council didn't show much of an appetite to put up the money. They talked about getting a Lottery grant to fund the renovation, but nothing ever came of it. It's a shame, really, because this is a beautiful piece of sculpture under all the grime.'

Everything Rhodri had told me spoke of a town that had given up on all the things that once made it attractive to visitors, defeated by lack of money and interest. But he retained a fondness for his hometown that I couldn't help but find endearing.

'I don't know about you,' I said, 'but I need something to take the taste of that water out of my mouth.'

We wandered back the way we'd come, until, among the cluster of shops at the pier head, we found a small booth selling candyfloss and freshly made popcorn. The savoury-sweet scents of hot syrup and corn mingled on the air. I watched as the girl behind the counter pushed waxed paper sticks into the machine, teasing the strands of sticky pink sugar into two soft clouds. When I'd paid for them, I handed one to Rhodri, and began to pick at the other, breaking off a piece of floss and popping it into my mouth. It dissolved on my tongue, and I sighed.

'Why do all the things that are really bad for you taste so good?' I wondered aloud.

'You know what we need to wash this down,' Rhodri replied. 'A nice glass of rosé. But are we going to drink it at your place, or mine?'

'Yours,' I blurted, thinking that I couldn't let him into my apartment; not when there might be something lying around that might alert him to the fact I wasn't the woman he believed me to be. Afraid my hasty response might have sounded suspicious, I added, 'Like I said, Dean and Bayo don't know I'm out with you. And their apartment is on the floor below mine. If we ran into them, it could be … awkward.'

'Yeah, I take your point.' He took another bite of his

candyfloss. 'But I need to warn you, I'm not the tidiest guy in the world.'

'Oh, don't worry. A little bit of clutter isn't going to put me off you.'

As we headed in the direction of the nearest off-licence to pick up a bottle of wine, I felt as though I'd averted some kind of mini-crisis. But how long could I keep on coming up with excuses to make sure Rhodri didn't find out I was really Claudia Anthony?

constable, you together with Nox... I'm off to the school
gym to do a bit...

"What's it, honey, a pile of crime... no reason to run
me around...

As soon as the doorman of all-...-over is forbidden
to plough a square of sand, I talk as though I've seen
some sort of tangent... "as I saw long until I walk," a
coming up was a cross to Mike sure Micah, didn't buy
one, water...?" I say, Adam...

170

THIRTEEN

Rhodri lived in the middle of a terrace of neat, stone houses, roofed with dark slate, which followed the line of a low, tree-covered hill. As he fumbled to put his key in the lock, I took in the ivy that clung to the front of the house, and the satellite dish fixed discreetly to a spot just below the guttering.

'Come in,' he said, pushing open the door and almost dragging me inside. 'Take a seat in the living room. I'll go get some glasses for this wine.'

His words were punctuated with quick, nibbling kisses, and instead of doing what he'd suggested, I followed him through to the kitchen, not wanting to be apart from him a second longer than I had to. Our anticipation had been building almost from the moment we'd picked up the bottle of sparkling rosé wine, and every moment we weren't twined together, kissing and caressing each other, was a moment too long.

Was it wrong to want any man as much as I wanted Rhodri? Especially when I knew that this could be nothing more than a passing romance, destined to end as soon as I stopped being Jane? If so, I didn't care.

Rhodri unwrapped the foil, and eased the cork out of

the bottle. The wine fizzed up, threatening to spill all over the wooden table, and he quickly poured a small amount into two glasses. When that had settled, he topped up our drinks, and handed a glass to me.

'That's really good,' I said once I'd taken a sip.

'Isn't it?' Rhodri agreed. 'But I thought you wanted to drink it in bed.'

'I don't know if I can wait that long. I mean, we'd have to take it all the way upstairs, and that seems like such a chore …'

I set down my glass, and fell into Rhodri's arms. Our mouths joined in a sweet, wine-flavoured kiss that grew more urgent as the temperature rose between us.

Rhodri plucked at the halter fastening of my dress. The tie came apart without too much effort, the gaudily patterned material falling down towards my waist and baring my breasts to him. While I fought to free him of his top, he worked on pulling the dress all the way off me. I stepped out of the crumpled heap of fabric, and stood before him in only my skimpy lace panties.

'You know,' I murmured, as he looked at where the damp underwear clung to me, outlining in tantalizing detail, 'I almost didn't bother wearing these tonight.'

'God, if you'd done that, we'd never have made it as far as the pier. I'd have had to drag you into my office and fucked you over the desk. I couldn't have stood the thought that you were bare beneath that dress.' He slid a hand into my panties, cupping my mound. The heat of his touch had me squirming against his fingers, needing more. 'So innocent on the surface, but underneath, so wanton …'

He almost tore the flimsy underwear in his haste to remove it. Once he had me naked, he hoisted me up, so I was sitting on the kitchen table. I gave a surprised little laugh as my bottom made contact with the cool, smooth wood, but even before I'd got used to being in this unusual position, Rhodri had dropped to the floor at my feet and was pushing my thighs apart with his palms.

'You're not –' I began, half shocked, half delighted at the thought of him taking me here, in the kitchen. For all he'd said about his lack of tidiness, as I glanced round the room I saw no dirty pots in the sink, no foodstuffs on the counters that hadn't been returned to the fridge once he'd finished making his breakfast. And hadn't I been the one who'd told him I was so eager I didn't want to wait till we got to the bedroom? Still, it felt so rude to be sitting on this old table, legs spread wide and every detail exposed to him.

I looked down at where he knelt. His jeans looked taut around his crotch, the faded denim straining to contain his arousal, but he made no move to unzip himself. For the moment, this was all about me, and lust pulsed through me, the slow, heavy beat centred in my core.

'You look so beautiful right now,' he said, reaching out to trace his fingers over my unfurling lips. 'Everything you have is mine. Mine to touch, mine to taste ...'

I thought he might start to lick me then, but instead he continued to explore with his fingers, pushing one, then a second up into me with almost shameful ease. As Rhodri thrust those digits in and out, his thumb rolled over my clit, and a wave of tension began to build in my belly. Needing to soothe the answering ache at the tips of my breasts, I cupped them and pinched my nipples. Sensation rippled down, connecting with the growing pressure between my legs, and I cried out. Rhodri paused, his fingers stilling their thrusting motion. I begged him to carry on, but instead he withdrew his hand and pulled it away.

'Don't stop now,' I whimpered, 'not when I'm so close.'

'Sweetheart, I've got no intention of stopping.' Those were the last words Rhodri spoke before he replaced his fingers with his hot, urgent mouth. Just the feel of his sighing breath against my mound had me gripping hard at his hair, urging him to lick harder, to concentrate on the spot that was the source of my pleasure. He worked with fast little flicks, like a cat lapping up milk, before running his tongue in one slow, lazy sweep from my clit to my rear hole.

My world turned upside-down as I tumbled over the edge of ecstasy, pushing myself hard against Rhodri's nose and mouth as I came. I rode the wave, feeling it crest again, more sharply than before, and then he gave one last, loving lick and my heartbeat began to slow towards normal.

It took me a few moments to find the words to thank him, and my legs were unsteady as he eased me down from the table and helped me to stand.

'And now let's go upstairs,' he said. 'Let me show you what I can do when I decide to take my time.'

We lay tangled in the one thin sheet that remained on Rhodri's bed. We'd pushed the rest of the covers to the floor, then I'd stripped Rhodri of his jeans and underwear and we'd made love with me on top, slowly riding his cock. Now, I was cradled in his arms, my head resting on his chest as I listened to the steady, calming beat of his heart.

'Jane, has it ever been like this with anyone else?' Rhodri murmured. They weren't the words I'd expected to hear as I drifted off to sleep, and instantly my senses were alert.

'What do you mean?'

'You must feel it. This … connection we have. Like we were always meant to be together, wherever we met and whatever our circumstances were. I know it's only been a couple of weeks, but I'm really falling for you.'

I didn't know how to respond. Inwardly, part of me rejoiced at Rhodri's declaration, knowing his feelings were as strong as mine. But I had to play this carefully, remind him of the reality of our situation.

'You're right, I think we could have something very special here,' I said at length. 'But don't you think this is all moving a little fast?'

'What are you saying; that you want me to back off?'

'Not at all,' I replied, hurt by the accusation. 'Rhodri, I've had a great evening tonight, that horrible spa water notwithstanding. I can't remember the last time I laughed so much. I love being with you, getting to see this town through your eyes. And the sex – we've been doing things I've only ever fantasised about before. But …' I felt the slight stiffening in his body as he reacted to the note of caution in my voice. 'I'm only going to be in Aberpentre for another couple of weeks, until we finish filming. After that, I have to go home, try and pick up my life back in the real world.'

'We could keep seeing each other. It's not like Caernarfon is on the other side of the world.'

He'd have had a point, if not for the fact that when I

talked about "home", I meant London.

'You're right, but things are more complicated than that.' No doubt he was hoping for me to elaborate, but I just couldn't tell him the truth. Instead, I continued, 'There'll be all the loose ends to tie up with the documentary, and I need to sort out my work situation. By which, I mean I need to find myself something permanent. After all, the bills don't pay themselves.'

'You could have that here, if you wanted. Tom's going to college in a few months, don't forget, and I'll be recruiting to fill his role. There might even be the possibility of temporary work before then: holiday cover for Morwenna and Tom. If your CV landed on my desk, I'd look at it very favourably.'

I thought back to what Angharad had said when she'd confronted me in the convenience store, her insinuation that I was only using Rhodri to get myself a job at the Anthony. 'That's a really tempting offer, and I'd have to think about it. But not right now. Let's enjoy the rest of the time we have together, and then we can talk about this again.'

I hoped my words had reassured him, as I snuggled up to him in the dark once more. I did want to be with him, despite what he might think, and the worst part was I couldn't let him know just how much.

FOURTEEN

Golden light peeped through a crack in the curtains. The display of the digital clock on the bedside table read 6.55. When I tried to sit up on the bed, knowing I needed to go home and get ready for another working day, Rhodri pulled me closer to him.

'Morning, gorgeous,' he murmured in my ear. His early-morning erection poked at my bum. 'Sleep well?'

'Mm,' I replied, fighting to come fully awake. 'But I hadn't realised it was so late. I have to go.'

'Don't, Jane.' Rhodri ran his fingers over the swell of my hip. 'Stay here with me. I'll make us both some breakfast …'

The idea was appealing, as was the knowledge that he was hard and ready for me once more, but I pushed his caressing hand away. 'I don't have a choice. Look, I'm not running out on you, if that's what you're worried about,' I said, thinking back to the doubts he'd voiced about relationship in the moments before we'd fallen asleep. 'I just can't go into work dressed in the stuff I was wearing last night, and all my uniform clothes are in my apartment.'

He conceded my point, but reached out to grab my

wrist as I made to slip out of bed. 'OK, but I want just one last kiss before you leave.'

I turned, and bent my head to his. Our lips met, and there was so much passion in his kiss that my resolve almost weakened. But even if Rhodri was only working a half-day today, I had to be at work on time. Morwenna would be expecting me to relieve her, and it wouldn't be fair to keep her waiting.

'I'll see you later.' I pulled free of him with some reluctance, and started to look for my clothes, before remembering I'd left them scattered on the kitchen floor. 'And don't forget, you're going to pick out that waistcoat for me.'

'Already sorted,' he replied. 'Hey, Jane, aren't you forgetting something?'

I turned to see he'd propped himself up on one elbow, the sheets rumpled around his waist. Half-expecting him to call me back so he could steal another kiss, I realised with a sick lurching in my stomach that he held my glasses in his other hand.

'Silly me. That's what happens when I'm in a rush. Sometimes I think I'd forget my head if it wasn't screwed on.' I reached out and took them from him. At least he'd resisted the temptation to try them on, as people so often did when they found a pair of spectacles belonging to a friend. If he'd discovered those were plain glass, not prescription lenses, I'd be facing some very difficult questions.

You only have to keep up this charade for another couple of weeks, I reminded myself. Just try not to think about what will happen after that.

Rhodri had been slightly off in his timings. I'd been expecting the wedding party to turn up at the hotel after I came off my shift on Reception. Instead, it was about quarter to four when the front doors opened and the first gaggle of guests – a group of twenty-somethings in lounge suits and pretty summer dresses – entered the lobby, laughing and chattering. If they were aware of Dean and his camera, recording their arrival, no one commented. From what I'd been told, no one had objected to the possibility of being filmed; as I'd always told Kay, everyone these days wants to be a star.

I directed them through to the hotel's function room, the Princess Alexandra Suite, which had been named for Edward VII's long-suffering wife. Earlier in the afternoon, I'd taken a moment to pop my head round the door and check on the preparations. The transformation was impressive. Crisp linen cloths and sparkling glassware gave the tables an elegant appearance, while swathes of gauzy white fabric draped around the central pillars, and bouquets of lilies standing in tall vases, brought an air of freshness to a room that had seemed shabby and old.

With a proper makeover, this suite could become a real asset to the hotel. In the plans Hammond had outlined to Dad, it had been the site of his health complex. I closed my eyes and tried to imagine the tables replaced with state of the art gym equipment, and mirrors on the walls so patrons could check their technique as they exercised – or simply check out the bodies of the people on the neighbouring treadmills. Blinking the image away, I'd returned to the reception area, wondering why the thought of people sitting and toasting the newlyweds seemed so much more attractive than using the space as a gym.

An older couple, who had to be the parents of either the bride or groom, walked into the lobby. They were followed by two bridesmaids: one a girl of around nine or ten and the other, who I took to be the maid of honour, in her early twenties. Bridesmaids' dresses have a reputation for being notoriously unflattering, so the bride stands no chance of being outshone, but these were of a fetching shade of scarlet that suited the girls' pale skin and dark brown hair.

Behind them came the bride and groom. He was a tall, thickset type who probably spent most Saturdays shoring up a rugby scrum, and looked as though he'd been squeezed into his sober black morning suit, which was accented by a tie the same colour as the bridesmaids' outfits. His wife was a good head shorter, in a strapless white dress that had a tight-fitting top and a frothy skirt, with subtle scarlet threads woven into the hem. Both had scraps of confetti clinging to their clothing, and matching, slightly dazed expressions, as though the significance of what they'd done was only now beginning to sink in.

'Mr and Mrs Jenkins.' I smiled at them both. 'Congratulations on your marriage. If you'd like to follow the signs to the Princess Alexandra Suite, someone will be waiting there to greet you.'

Mr Jenkins nodded his thanks at me, and put an arm round his new wife to steer her in the direction of the suite. She seemed dainty, almost bird-like in comparison to him, and his gesture seemed both protective and loving. I felt a strange pang of envy as I watched them walk away.

'You all right, Jane?'

I turned my head at the sound of Tom's voice. He'd set his headphones down on the front counter, and was tightening the knot in his tie, readying himself for duty.

'Fine, thanks, Tom. Unless there are any stragglers who've got lost on the way, I think all the wedding guests have arrived. If anyone else does turn up, send them through to the function room. I've got to go to Rhodri's office, pick up my outfit.' I shrugged out of my jacket as I spoke. 'He's got me working as part of the wait staff this afternoon.'

'Rather you than me.' He grinned. 'No, seriously, I'm sure you'll do a grand job. And I don't suppose there's any chance of you sneaking me out a slice of wedding cake, is there? Only I love marzipan ...'

I had to admire his cheek. 'I'll see what I can do, but I'm not promising anything.'

'Thanks, Jane. You rock.'

Leaving Tom to set up for his shift, I went down the corridor and knocked on Rhodri's office door. When he called, 'Enter,' I stepped inside, to see the waistcoat he'd picked out for me on a hanger that dangled from the coat stand.

'This should be your size,' he said, taking it down and handing it to me. I slipped it on, and buttoned it up. It was a little snug, but the next size up would have been too loose on me.

'You look great,' Rhodri said. 'Though it would be even better if you lost the blouse. Maybe the bra too.'

'Hey, that's enough of that,' I warned him, even though he'd set my mind racing with thoughts of being dressed the way he suggested. He'd stand before me, slowly unbuttoning the waistcoat and gradually revealing my bare breasts to his greedy gaze ...

With some effort, I snapped back to reality.

181

'Now, you know where you need to be and what you have to do?' he enquired.

'Of course. I'm to report to Ian, the head waiter, and he'll assign me my duties.'

'Good. I'll try and drop in on you before I leave tonight, see how you're getting on.'

I paused with my hand on the door handle. 'Tom's asked me to get him some cake, if I can. You don't want a piece while I'm at it, do you?'

He shook his head. 'Thanks, but no. Though they do say that if you put a little bit of wedding cake under your pillow when you go to bed, you'll dream about the person you're going to marry.' His gaze met mine, and I looked away quickly.

'I never had you as the superstitious type, Rhodri. And I'd better go, or they'll be wondering why they're still short of a waitress.'

Before I could turn to leave, Rhodri caught me by the hand and dropped a kiss, rich with intent, on my lips. I could have stayed there all too easily, melting into his arms and surrendering to my desire for him – a desire that seemed to burn brighter with every passing day. But I steeled myself and pulled away. I had a job to do. Pleasure could wait, and when it came, it would be all the sweeter for having been delayed.

The Princess Alexandra Suite, so quiet and serene earlier in the afternoon, now buzzed with activity. The wedding party were assembled at the long table that had been set up on a raised dais by the far wall, and the guests had taken their places at the half-dozen round tables occupying the area on the edges of the dance floor, studying the menus, taking photographs of each other and talking in loud, excited voices. The waiting staff, in their neat black and white uniforms, were busy filling wine glasses and offering bread rolls from wicker baskets.

Dean and Bayo patrolled the perimeter of the room, filming the action, though I doubted whether much of this footage would make the final cut. Knowing Dean and his penchant for outrageous documentary ideas, I reckoned he'd be hoping for a fight to break out, or the bride to get hideously drunk and flash her knickers, so he could pitch *When Wedding Receptions Go Bad*.

Taking a moment to compose myself, I then headed over to get my instructions. I'd been introduced briefly to the chubby, fair-haired Ian in the week, and though he appeared calm, even laidback, on the surface, I'd been told by Rhodri that he ran his dining room with almost military precision.

'Hi, Ian. Where do you need me?'

'Jane, thanks again for helping us out. You'll be covering Tables three and four, along with Kerry and Joe. If you go through to the kitchen –' he indicated in the direction of a pair of swing doors to our right '– the starters are ready to be brought out. Smoked salmon mousse or wild mushroom terrine.'

No soup. I heaved a huge inward sigh of relief. With any luck, these starter options would be plated up and ready to go, meaning very little chance of me spilling something on an unsuspecting guest.

When I walked into the kitchen, just as I'd hoped, I was greeted by two rows of plates, one containing neat quenelles of creamy pink mousse and the other slices of a dark, savoury terrine. My stomach rumbled, and I wished

I'd thought to snack on a power bar before starting my waitressing stint.

'You're on terrines,' one of the white-jacketed cooks said without looking up at me.

My squeaked, 'Yes, chef,' seemed to be the correct response. I picked up two of the small white china plates, copying the technique I'd seen during my internet research. The first plate I held with the thumb over the rim, with my index and middle fingers under the plate, holding it steady. The second plate was supported by the tips of my ring and little fingers, the base of my thumb and lower forearm. I trusted that my grip was secure enough, and followed one of the other waitresses, who appeared to be on mousse duty, out of the kitchen.

By the time I'd served the first couple of diners on Table three and returned for a second pair of plates, most of my nerves had evaporated. Though the guests were largely engrossed in their own conversations, all paused for long enough to answer my question of, "Mousse or terrine?", and to thank me if I placed the appropriate choice in front of them. Whether they'd be quite so polite and appreciative by the time they'd had a glass or two of wine, I didn't know, but as yet, no one seemed to have realised I was a total novice when it came to waiting tables.

Soon, the conversation had become more muted, and the loudest sound in the room was the chink of cutlery on china. That was always a good sign, when diners had their full attention claimed by their food.

'So what do we do about clearing away the plates?' I asked as I passed Ian.

'You wait until everyone at the table has finished

eating, and then you start,' he told me. 'If in doubt, just watch and follow everyone else. But relax, Jane; you're doing OK so far.'

The main course choices were slow roasted saddle of Welsh lamb or pearl barley and root vegetable risotto. The staff serving the risotto had by far the easier task, as it had already been ladled into shallow soup plates. I, however, found myself with a tray of thick lamb slices, drizzled with a rich red wine jus, which I had to portion out to each guest in turn. All the while, as I tried not to splash either the diners or myself with errant flecks of the jus, I was aware of Dean, his lens trained on me. For the first time in more years than I could remember, I was mastering a skill for which my extensive training in hotel work had not prepared me, and I felt bizarrely proud of myself by the time I returned to the kitchen with the last of the empty meat platters.

'Oh God,' one of the other girls was complaining, as she returned with a serving dish that held a few scraps of dauphinoise potatoes. 'Why do I always get the table with the single friends of the groom? Filthy buggers can't keep their hands off my bum …'

I smiled to myself, thinking that at least I'd escaped that particular ordeal. Though I was convinced Hugo Murray would love some shots of me dealing with a drink-fuelled, well-meaning groper.

Once Kerry and I had cleared away the remains of the main course, along with any cutlery apart from that needed for dessert, we took a minute to brush the tablecloths clean of crumbs, while Joe was kept busy making sure the guests' wine glasses were refilled.

By the time we'd served dessert – white chocolate

delice with raspberries or Welsh rarebit with red onion chutney – my feet were aching, even in the sensible, low-heeled shoes I wore, and I could have happily popped out for some fresh air. But we had to make sure that the champagne glasses were charged and ready for the impending toasts, and then there was the small matter of serving tea and coffee. Whatever the waiting staff were earning for putting in these extra hours today, they deserved every penny of it.

As I returned from taking the dessert plates back to the kitchen and took up my post between tables three and four, the bride's father was rising to his feet. He rattled a teaspoon against his wine glass, attracting the attention of everyone in the room. Once an expectant silence had settled, he launched into his speech. 'Ladies and gentlemen, I'd like to thank you all for coming to the wedding of Mike and Leanne. It seems like only five minutes since my little girl …'

'Hey, how's it going?' Rhodri's voice was soft in my ear.

Engrossed in my work, I'd forgotten that he'd promised to check in on me. 'Going well, I think. I could do with a glass of what they're drinking –' I nodded my head in the direction of a couple of guests who were sipping their champagne '– but so far I've got through this without any disasters. Whoever's responsible for the catering has done a fantastic job.'

'It's all the work of the regular guys in the kitchen. Because we took this wedding on at such short notice, we knew we'd have to go with the food choices the couple had already asked their guests to decide on. In future, though, Jean-Luc, the head chef, is going to have more freedom in designing his own menu.'

Rhodri was so close behind me I could have taken a step back and let my body press up against his. But that would hardly have been prudent, not with Ian's beady eyes on me, and Dean hovering so close with his camera. For all I knew, Bayo was picking up every word of our conversation, and I needed to keep up the pretence that my relationship with Rhodri was a purely professional one.

'So you think this event has been a success?' I spoke a little louder, and this time I was sure my words would be captured by the microphone.

'I'm quietly confident,' he replied. 'And I'd like to think it will be the first of many. You know, Jane, it's strange, but since you arrived here, I've started seeing this hotel in a whole new light. Before, I wasn't entirely sure it had a future. Now, I'm convinced it does.'

I said nothing, knowing the boys had a perfect soundbite from Rhodri and anything I added would be superfluous.

At the top table, the bride's father had finished his speech and the groom was stumbling through a few words, gazing at his new wife from time to time with the expression of a man clearly besotted. My mind flashed back to Kay and Paul's wedding. I'd seen that same look on Paul's face when he'd taken Kay out on to the floor for their first dance together.

I glanced at Rhodri, wondering what he might be thinking at this moment.

'Jane.' When I turned at the sound of the voice, I saw Ian looking at me. 'I need you to clear away the tea and coffee cups from your tables. Once that's done, start removing any empty wine and champagne glasses. If the guests need any further drinks, they'll be getting those themselves from the bar.'

'Of course. Right away.' I smiled at Rhodri. 'I'll see you later.'

With that, I scurried away to help Kerry and Joe with the clear-up operation. Serving of the regular evening meal would begin at 6.30 in the hotel dining room, and most of the waiting staff would be moving over in preparation for that. At least my duties would be over for the day – but then, I had already put in a full shift on the front desk.

The best man had taken the floor by now. Though I wasn't paying too much attention, I heard enough to know that now and then he slipped from English to Welsh. Every time he did, he was greeted with a loud roar of laughter from the group of friends whose wandering hands I'd heard the waitress complain about. Was he deliberately choosing to make comments he knew some of the guests might not understand, or did jokes just sound naturally filthier in Welsh?

When he finally sat down, to a huge round of cheers and applause and a hearty slap on the back from the groom, Ian walked into the middle of the dance floor. He waited until he had everyone's full attention.

'Ladies and gentlemen, Mr and Mrs Jenkins will now cut the cake.'

A couple of squeals of delight went up from among the guests, and people rushed to grab their cameras and fight for the best spots to take a snap of the action. I'd seen the cake when I'd visited the suite earlier in the afternoon; three tiers high, it had figures designed to represent the happy couple on top, as was traditional. Except that in this case, the groom wore not the usual morning suit and top hat, but a scarlet rugby jersey and white shorts.

The bride and groom posed for photographs, both of them holding the knife as they pressed to the bottom tier of the cake. Then, with one steady downward stroke, they sliced through the thick, white icing.

When they stepped aside, a couple of the waitresses moved in, to start the process of cutting the cake into segments and lay it on paper plates to be handed round to the guests.

I stretched, rolling my shoulders to ease the slight stiffness in my neck. All the tension I'd been carrying, so afraid that I might drop a wine glass or dump food in a guest's lap, was released as I exhaled a long, slow breath.

I walked over to Ian, hoping that he would now let me off further duty. 'The table's clear. Will you need me to do anything else?'

'No, I think that's it. Thank you for your help this afternoon, Jane, particularly at such short notice.'

'You're welcome. And in a funny way, I think I actually enjoyed myself.'

He smiled, and seemed about to respond. Then someone called his name from the doorway that led through to the kitchen, and he excused himself.

Before I could leave the function room, Rhodri wandered over and handed me something wrapped in a white paper napkin. When I opened it up, I saw a small square of fruitcake, encased in marzipan and royal icing. He smiled at me. 'I saw you were busy, so I went to get some of this for you. I'm taking another piece out for Tom.'

'Thanks, but you really didn't need to,' I said, wrapping

189

the cake up securely once more. 'I'm sure I'd have found the time.'

'You've worked hard today, Jane. Don't feel like you always have to do everything for everyone.' He lowered his voice, and looked straight into my eyes. 'Have sweet dreams tonight.'

FIFTEEN

I didn't place the wedding cake beneath my pillow that night. Not because I have a healthy distrust of superstition, but because I was so peckish that I'd polished it off even before I walked up the front steps to the Bay Vista apartments.

Even without any outside assistance, I dreamed of Rhodri, though not in the way I might have wished. I saw myself standing outside a beautiful Norman church, dressed in a slim-fitting white gown with a long, flowing train, and with a veil over my head. My father stood beside me, looking handsome in top hat and tails, preparing to give me away. The ushers opened the front door, and the strains of Mendelssohn's 'Wedding March' floated out on the air. We began our slow procession down the aisle, to where I knew Rhodri stood waiting for me. In the pews on either of me stood friends, family, work colleagues, my old school classmates – it seemed like everyone I'd ever known was here, looking on and murmuring to each other as I passed. But even before I'd gone a few steps, I became aware that Rhodri wasn't alone at the altar. Beside him was a figure in an identical dress to mine. As I approached, she turned to face me, throwing back her veil, and I saw that Rhodri's bride was Angharad.

The vision jolted me awake. I sat up, and grabbed for my phone, to check the time on the display. Just before one o'clock. I'd been asleep a little over an hour. With a sigh, I rolled over and closed my eyes, only to see Angharad, smug with triumph, as she pushed the gauzy fabric away from her face. Knowing I wouldn't get back to sleep for a while, I went and heated up a mug of milk, sweetened it with honey, then took it through to the living room. I channel-surfed until I found an old episode of *Man v. Food*, and settled down to watch the presenter attempt to eat a burger that was bigger than his own head.

My Sundays off had become precious time, enabling me to catch up on all the chores I neglected in the week, but this morning I had other things on my mind. At least when I'd nodded off again, clutching the silly little stuffed rabbit that Rhodri had won for me, my sleep had been dreamless. But that image of Angharad claiming Rhodri as her husband still lingered in my subconscious? Why did I care so much? It was only a stupid nightmare, brought on by all the anxieties that had beset me when I'd thought I was going to muck up my spell of silver service waitressing. In reality, I'd passed that test without a hitch. Maybe I should treat the dream as a sign that whatever life threw at me, even a resentful ex-girlfriend, I could cope with it.

Of more immediate concern was the future of the hotel. Every time I began to question whether there any point in keeping it as a going concern, something happened to make me rethink my plans. There was no doubt that hosting the wedding reception yesterday had been a clever move on Rhodri's part. I hadn't discussed with him the price he'd charged for the venue, or the costs involved in employing the waiting staff outside their usual hours, and I was sure he'd have found it strange if I had. But I liked the fact he was trying to bring in new sources of revenue, and I was keen to see how other local hotels managed to do the same thing.

Finding that out should be easy enough. Reaching for my laptop, I opened the browser. I called up one of the best-known holiday review sites, and typed "Aberpentre" into the "choose location" box. Immediately, numbers one to twenty in a total list of thirty-one results appeared, ranked by popularity. The Anthony came in at a not so distinguished thirteen. Unlucky for me, I thought.

When I looked more closely at the listings, almost half of those that scored above the Anthony were either bed and breakfast establishments or self-catered holiday cottages. Not quite the market we were aiming to compete with, and I knew I could safely discount them, but it meant there were still half a dozen hotels gaining higher ratings from those who stayed there.

I turned my attention instead to the top-rated establishment, The Coron. I knew the place by sight, with its pale pink façade and sloping gables, but from the outside at least, it looked no different to any of half a dozen similar hotels along the sea front. Scrolling through the comments that had been left, I saw guests had praised the "friendly service", "comfortable rooms", and "delicious, full Welsh breakfast". The Anthony offered all those things, at very similar prices, and as Rhodri had said, it had a long-standing reputation as the finest hotel in the area. Why then, I wondered, did so many people opt for The Coron?

Reading further, I noticed several references to the afternoon tea served by the hotel; something which was, apparently, available to non-residents too. Now, that sounded like something I ought to be checking out – and not just because I'd always been partial to scones with clotted cream and a pot of Earl Grey tea.

A visit to The Coron's own website provided more details, along with a phone number. The opportunity for a spot of hands-on research was too much to resist. When I dialled the hotel, my call was answered by a personable-sounding girl who announced herself as Magda and was more than happy to take my booking. Tea for three, on Tuesday afternoon at half-past four. For an extra five pounds per head, she informed me, I could upgrade to what she called the "sparkling tea", which included a glass of Prosecco.

'You know,' I said, 'that sounds really good. Yes, I'll go for it.' I scribbled a reference to the offer on my notepad.

Next, I rang Dean's number. When he answered, I heard noises in the background that sounded like heavy artillery fire, and I heard him shout at Bayo to turn the volume down.

'Everything OK there?' I asked.

'Oh, he's just treated himself to the latest *Walking Dead* game. He's spent all morning shooting everything that shambles.' Dean heaved a theatrical sigh.

'Well, speaking of treats, I've lined up something that should be more to your liking. I'm taking you and Bayo for afternoon tea on Tuesday afternoon.'

'What's the occasion?'

'Nothing special. I'm just doing a bit of extra-curricular research. I want to see where this hotel is getting it wrong and other places are getting it right. Not just here, but I need to make sure people think of the Anthony chain as their first choice destination.' There was another, fainter explosion, followed by an answering yell of triumph from Bayo. 'I'm starting to sound like a press release, aren't I?'

'Not at all, babe,' Dean assured me. 'But thank you for the invitation. I'll let Bayo know about it when he stops blowing the heads off zombies.'

I'd lied when I told Dean that Tuesday wasn't a special occasion. In truth, it was my birthday. But when the Wild Card team had concocted Jane Ennis's fake CV, someone's finger had slipped on the keyboard, and now everyone believed I'd been born in July, Dean and Bayo included. I had to bite my lip and say nothing, afraid if that little lie came to light, the bigger ones would tumble out after it.

At least Kay had remembered. I had an animated card from her waiting in my inbox when I checked my emails at breakfast, along with a gift voucher for a day at a health spa in the New Forest. Messages of congratulation had turned up from a couple of other friends too, and I made a mental note to catch up with them when I was back in London. Last year, I'd taken the whole day off, and Kay and I had taken the train down to Brighton, where we'd browsed in the quirky shops in The Lanes, had lunch at a little French bistro, and taken a tour of the Royal Pavilion. Today, I had a full shift on the front desk at the Anthony to look forward to.

Knowing she'd be on her regular commute from Richmond into central London, I fired off a text to her.

Thanks for my present. Will need some pampering when this month is up ☺

Her reply was instant. *Any time, darling. Are you doing anything nice with your man tonight?*

I knew she referred to Rhodri.

He's not my man – and he doesn't know it's my birthday. Long story. Will explain when I see you, I promise.

I went to dump the breakfast dishes in the sink, and prepared to leave for work. At least I had tea with the boys to look forward to, I reminded myself.

Still, I caught myself glancing at the clock on the lobby wall every few minutes, convinced that time had slowed to a halt. The most excitement I had all day was helping a family from Austin, Texas find a suitable restaurant for lunch. When the father made some comment about not being able to find a decent burger anywhere in town, I was able to recommend the Caffi Memphis without hesitation. Of course, that set me thinking about the evening I'd spent there with Rhodri, when the initial frostiness between us had begun to thaw.

At last, I looked up to see Tom sauntering into the hotel. Even before he'd reached the front desk, I was out of my seat and heading for the lockers.

'Hot date tonight?' he commented, when I emerged from the staff cloakroom a few moments later in the same maxidress and gladiator sandals I'd worn for my Friday night out with Rhodri.

I shook my head. 'I'm off for afternoon tea with those two –' I gestured to Bayo and Dean, who had been lounging on one of the low sofas in the lobby, waiting for me.

They rose from their seats as I approached. I'd asked them to leave their equipment at home. Requesting

196

permission to film in The Coron would have resulted in a series of questions I preferred not to answer. Today of all days, I just wanted to kick back and have some fun.

'OK, well, have a good time,' Tom said. 'Don't do anything I wouldn't.'

I put my fingers to my lips and blew him a kiss, then followed the lads out of the front door.

'So why The Coron?' Dean asked, as he dodged a group of small boys in school uniform who were running along their pavement, whirling their gym bags around their heads as they went.

'It's the top hotel in town, according to all the review sites, at least. And people really seem to like the teas they provide. Plus I know you boys like your cake.' I grinned. 'Speaking of which, Bayo, has Gaynor brought you any more of her baking recently?'

He looked sheepish for a moment, then said, 'If you must know, she gave me some *bara brith* for my lunchbox.'

I knew he referred to the tea bread that was common across Wales, rich with dried fruit and candied peel. 'Nice?'

'Very. I know we joke about it, but damn, the woman can bake.'

An idea popped into my head. If Gaynor Rhys really was as good a cook as Bayo claimed, maybe she could be persuaded to supply her baked goods for the Anthony, if we ever got as far as instating afternoon tea. I kept the thought to myself. Everything concerning the hotel was ifs and buts right now.

When we walked into the lobby of The Coron, the difference from my current working environment was marked. The place was much smaller, but it had a light, airy feel, enhanced by the fact the walls had obviously been painted at some time in the last few months. The dark blue carpet, with its subtle pattern of gold crowns that alluded to the hotel's name, looked new, and there were comfortable-looking brown leather chesterfields arranged around a large, inlaid table.

The woman on the front desk, whose name badge told me she was the Magda I'd spoken to on the phone, greeted me with a wide smile. I gave my name to her, and she looked up my reservation in moments. No waiting for a computer that might or might not decide to offer up the information without crashing; no need to apologise for a system that was slow to load.

'We're a little early,' I said. 'I hope that's not a problem.'

'Not at all, Miss Ennis. Your table should be ready for you now, if you'd all like to follow me to the dining room.'

Magda led us up a flight of three wide stairs and along a hallway. At the door of the dining room, we were met by a girl in a neat, all-black outfit of shirt, slacks, and waistcoat.

'Please come through.' Like Magda, she spoke with a noticeable Eastern European accent, and I wondered about The Coron's recruitment policy. Much of the hotel industry had come to rely on foreign employees. The standard line was that they were prepared to work harder than the local population, and had less of a problem with unsociable hours, but I knew hand in hand with that went a willingness to work for well below the minimum wage, and to make less of a fuss if they were badly treated by their bosses.

The waitress showed us to a corner table. Of the other ten or so tables in the room, around half were occupied, mostly by groups of two or three women who gossiped as they spread cream on a scone, or poured themselves another cup of tea.

Once we were seated, she asked, 'Would you like Assam tea, Earl Grey, or Welsh Breakfast?'

As one, the three of us agreed that we would try the last one. 'When in Wales ...,' Bayo said with a smile, as the waitress made a note on her pad.

'And would you like me to bring your Prosecco before you have your tea?'

'You never told us there was going to be fizz,' Dean said.

'Only the best for you,' I assured him. To the girl, I said, 'Yes, if you could bring it now that would be lovely, thank you.'

She nodded, and went to retrieve a bottle that stood chilling in a silver bucket on a thin, elegant stand. Once she'd poured us each a glass, she disappeared in what I assumed to be the direction of the kitchen.

I raised my glass. 'Dean, congratulations again on your impending wedding.'

He thanked me again, and we all sipped at our drinks.

'Well, this is very nice,' he said, looking around the room.

'Isn't it?' I replied. 'And it's something that could so easily be brought in at the Anthony. All it takes is a willingness on the part of a few people.'

'I'm surprised you don't offer it already,' Bayo commented.

'We do, but only in what I'd call the flagship hotels. The one on the Strand, of course. Brighton, Bournemouth …' I broke off as the waitress arrived at our table with a three-tiered china cake stand. On the top tier was a selection of dainty sandwiches, cut into triangles and with their crusts removed. On the second were three scones, pots of jam in assorted flavours, and a dish of clotted cream. The bottom tier held mini éclairs and petits fours.

While I took mental notes, wondering whether I would replace the ham sandwiches with smoked salmon, or offer a more varied selection of cakes, the boys dug into the food. Tonight, I would sit down with the video camera and get my thoughts in some kind of order. Looking around The Coron's dining room, I saw how the Anthony could be given a new lease of life; become once more the desirable location it had been a century ago. All I had to do was persuade the board of directors it would be money well spent.

Filled with renewed enthusiasm for the whole project, I reached for an éclair.

SIXTEEN

My phone buzzed as I was leaving the sandwich shop. When I pulled it out of my pocket, I was surprised to see a text from Rhodri.

Course has finished earlier than I expected. Fancy going out tonight?

For the last two days, he'd been at Cardiff University, attending a Health and Safety refresher course. The company required all our hotel managers to have the necessary skills to cope in any emergency, which included knowledge basic first aid and how to act as a fire marshal. Training in risk assessment had also become a necessary part of the job, and so Rhodri had been sent off at our expense to make sure his knowledge in all these areas was up to date. Given that he'd have a four-hour drive back to Aberpentre, I'd already written off any chance of spending the evening with him.

I'd love to, I replied.

OK, see you at 7 p.m. outside the Anthony.

'What's put a grin on your face?' Dean asked, as I handed him the ham and coleslaw bap he'd ordered. Even though I'd told him and Bayo there was little point in their hanging around, particularly with Rhodri away, they'd spent most of the morning sitting in the lobby, drinking coffee and reading the papers.

'Oh nothing.' I hadn't even been aware I was smiling until he'd pointed it out. Did Rhodri really have such an obvious effect on me? 'Just pleased that it's Friday, that's all. It's been a long week.'

'I know what you mean,' he said. 'If time flies when you're having fun, what does it mean when it drags?'

'Don't worry, mate,' Bayo reassured him. 'Only another week and a bit to go, and then we wave bye-bye to Aberpentre.'

'Do you have another job lined up when this one finishes?' I asked. From what Hugo Murray had told me of Wild Card, I knew they mostly produced shows for Channels four and five, and they could be sent just about anywhere in the world, depending on the subject matter.

'Yeah, we're off to Ayia Napa, following a bunch of lads from Manchester for *Sun, Sex and Stag Parties*. I mean, we joke about it now, but a couple of days on the lash with them and we're going to wish we were right back here, watching the paint peel off the walls …'

When I arrived back at the hotel at quarter past seven, there was no sign of Rhodri. I'd been delayed by a phone call as I'd been about to leave the apartment. Expecting it to be Rhodri, I'd answered without checking the caller display, only to find myself talking to Pete Ashton. He'd been calling for an update on the "good night's sleep" kits. Just the mention of those specially created eye masks had me thinking back to lying on Rhodri's lap, blindfolded and anxiously awaiting the next slap on my bottom. The image sent a delicious shiver of arousal through me, but it didn't explain why Pete was ringing me on Friday evening. I told him I had somewhere to be, and he apologised, telling me that he was in New York and had forgotten about the time difference. I ended the call as quickly as I could, promising that I'd fill Pete in on the reaction to the kits when I was back in London in ten days' time. I hated keeping anyone waiting – Dad had always drilled into me that it was a sign of bad manners – and I'd rehearsed my apology as I ran down the front steps of Bay Vista.

I looked up and down the street, trying to spot that familiar, dark-haired figure. Had Rhodri decided I'd stood him up? He couldn't think so little of me, surely.

Just as I was reaching for my phone to call him, a black Land Rover pulled up in front of me. The passenger window rolled down. I hoped no one was intending to ask me directions; I'd been here over a fortnight, and I still didn't know what half the streets in the area were called.

'Hey, Jane.' Rhodri smiled at me from the driver's seat. 'I'm really sorry. I thought I'd be here sooner, but the traffic coming through Merthyr was a nightmare.'

'That's OK, I've only just got here myself,' I admitted. 'Sorry, I just wasn't expecting you to be in a car, that's all.' In all the time I'd been working with Rhodri, I'd only ever seen him arriving at the hotel on foot. Given that it was only a twenty-minute walk from his home, I assumed he reckoned it wasn't worth all the expense and hassle of owning a car. Or maybe that attitude had been shaped by my own experience of London, where black cabs and the Tube took me everywhere I needed to go.

'Borrowed it from my dad,' he said. 'If I'd had to use the train, I wouldn't have got back till nearly midnight.'

'So, do you need to drop it off with him before we can

203

go anywhere?'

He shook his head. 'I said I'd drop it off to be valeted before I start work tomorrow, and take it back to him on Sunday. It was one of the conditions for him letting me use it.' I waited for him to continue, convinced there was some story behind that comment. Instead, he said, 'It means it's all mine till then. And I was thinking, I know the perfect place to take you tonight. Hop in.'

I did as he asked, dropping my bag on the wide console between the two front seats. As Rhodri indicated and pulled out into the flow of traffic, I adjusted my seat belt.

'So, where are we going?'

He smiled, and gave his head a little shake. 'You'll see.'

When he pressed a button on the dashboard, the Land Rover's interior filled with soft music: some female singer whose voice I didn't recognise. The tune was slow, soulful, and I settled back to enjoy the ride.

At Rhodri took the road that led out of town, I thought he might be heading for Castell Aberpentre. But he continued on, past the headland and down a gently sloping road that led to a small layby, big enough for only a couple of cars to park in. He killed the engine, though the music continued to play.

'Where are we?' I asked.

'I don't think this place has a name,' he replied. 'I've just always known it as "the bay". It's certainly not on any of the tourist maps, which should mean that we have the place to ourselves.'

Having switched off the music, he unbuckled his seat belt and got out of the vehicle. I followed suit, stepping out onto gravel chippings that crunched beneath my feet.

'Come with me.' Rhodri took my hand and led me down to the beach. There were no steps here: just a path that had been worn between the grassy dunes. The loose dirt shifted beneath my feet and I was glad I hadn't worn high heels tonight.

Once we were on the beach, I stopped to slip off my sandals, unable to resist the temptation to walk barefoot on the sand. We had another couple of hours before the sun went down, and the sea was still as glass, barely a ripple breaking the surface as the waves lapped gently at the shore.

'It's beautiful here,' I said, walking over to join Rhodri where he stood at the water's edge. 'So unspoilt.'

'Yeah, I keep forgetting how lucky I am to have this place pretty much on my doorstep. When I was in the sixth form, this was always where you came with that special girl you really wanted to impress.'

'So, did you ever bring anyone here?'

He stooped to pick up a large, flat stone, and sent it skimming across the tops of the waves. 'No. You needed a car, unless you had a mate who could be persuaded to double up on a date. I failed my test the first three times I took it, didn't pass it till I was nineteen. And by then, I'd found other ways of impressing the girls I wanted to be with.'

'That sounds remarkably mature.'

'Oh, not at all.' He shrugged. 'And tonight, after two days of sitting in a classroom learning about defining hazard and risk, and what to do to help someone who's choking on a piece of food, I just thought coming here might clear my head. Remind me of what's important to me. *Who's* important ...'

He looked into my eyes, and I rose up on my toes to stop his words with a kiss. Rhodri pulled me to him, and we went through the slow, delicious process of reacquainting ourselves with each other's lips. Every time I found myself in his arms, I wondered how I managed to find the strength to break away, when all I wanted to do was spend forever locked in an embrace, touching and tasting him.

At last, we came up for air, my lips already swollen and tingling from the force of his kisses. He brushed strands of hair from my face with gentle fingers.

'The last couple of nights, all I've dreamed of is you,' he murmured. 'I just couldn't wait to be with you again. To hold you close. To make love to you …'

As he pressed against me, I felt his cock press at me, hard and urgent, reinforcing his words. If he wanted to take me, here on this deserted beach, I had no desire to resist him.

My hands worked their way under his shirt to the smooth, warm skin beneath. Rhodri caressed the planes of my back and shoulders through my thin, sleeveless top. My nipples felt enormous, needing to be touched, needing Rhodri's fingers to touch them. When he pinched them, rolling the hard points in tight circles, he sent an electric current along my nerve-endings, igniting the fire inside me. I couldn't prevent a needy little whimper slipping from my lips, and I looked at Rhodri with mute appeal.

He chuckled, obviously all too aware of the state I'd been reduced to by his kisses and caresses.

'God, I need you so much,' he said. 'I don't know what it is about you, Jane, but you just make it so hard for me to control myself.'

'Then don't. You know you're not asking me to do anything I don't want to.'

'Let's go back to mine,' he suggested. 'I don't know about you, but I've never been a fan of sex on the beach. I find getting sand in all the wrong places kind of kills the mood.'

He didn't even give me time to put my sandals back on, half-dragging me up the path through the dunes in his haste to get me home. We only made it back as far as the Land Rover before his hands were all over me again.

Rhodri pushed me up against the driver's door, my bare shoulders making contact with the sun-warmed metal. I grabbed fistfuls of my own hair and threw my head back, thrusting my breasts forward as I did. In response, Rhodri moaned and pulled down the straps of my top, tugging at it and my bra till my tits were bared to him.

He latched on to my nipple, sucking hard and almost making me slither down the side of the car, so strong was my reaction. We were relatively secluded, shielded from the road by a line of trees, though there were gaps through which the driver of some passing car might be able to spot us. I didn't care if that happened. Nothing mattered apart from the feel of Rhodri's mouth, and the steady, growing ache between my legs. An ache I yearned for him to soothe.

Rhodri spun me round, so my breasts were pressed against the vehicle's big window. I almost wished there was someone on the other side of the glass to enjoy the view. I'd never had fantasies about being watched before, but the thought of performing for some anonymous voyeur had me more turned on than I could have imagined.

Some devilish impulse had told me not to bother with

underwear tonight, and Rhodri's eyes widened as he reached under my skirt and ran a hand up to the top of my thigh, where he found not the cotton and lace he'd clearly been expecting, but hot, wet, female flesh.

'You didn't ...' he breathed.

'You like it?' I asked.

He nodded. 'If I had my way, I'd make you leave your panties off all the time, so you'd always be ready for me.'

As he spoke, he ran his fingers over my soft, bare lips. He pushed first one, then a second deep inside, thrusting them in and out. The rude, wet sounds he made, and the ease with which his digits had entered me, told us both just how ready I was. I ground down harder on his hand, feeling my pleasure build. This was good, but not as good as having that big, hard cock of his inside me.

Rhodri opened the back door, and we almost tumbled inside the vehicle. Here, we had room to make ourselves comfortable. While he stripped out of his clothes, I kicked off my skirt, and sat on the back seat, skimming my fingers over myself.

Rhodri paused, his shirt halfway off, to watch me. 'Keep doing that, Jane, and I swear I'll come right now.'

I just smirked and carried on, keeping my desire on a steady simmer. Though in truth, just the sight of Rhodri's cock, jutting up as it came free of his confining underwear, was enough to give me all the stimulation I could ever need.

He fished a condom from his wallet, and skinned it down his shaft. Then he came and joined me, sitting on the soft, caramel-coloured leather seat and encouraging me to climb on to his lap. I held myself poised above his thick, round crest, preparing myself for the moment when it

208

would stretch me wide. Rhodri gazed up at me, silently willing me on.

I sank down, letting him fill me to the hilt. By now, I should have been used to the sensation, but each time it hit me afresh. We were connected, body and soul, and it seemed like no one could tear us apart.

'This moment …' I breathed. 'I never want it to end.'

Rhodri said nothing, just gave a low groan as I began to shift up and down. As I rode him, he reached up to cup my breasts, rubbing my nipples with his thumbs. There was no need for words; our eyes were locked together as we asserted our lust for each other, and I knew he was enjoying this every bit as much as I was. I took my time, guiding us both to the brink before stilling my movements so I could drop soft kisses on Rhodri's upturned face.

He grabbed my bum cheeks, encouraging me to move faster. I ground myself down on him, feeling the friction in all the right places as our bodies pressed together. At last, his hips were rising to meet my thrusts, and with a long drawn out groan, he reached his release. My own followed seconds later, and I slumped against his chest, burying my face in the crook of his neck.

'I'm so glad I didn't come here with anyone before,' Rhodri said, and I knew he was referring to his previous girlfriends. 'It could never have been as special as this.'

'Well, I'm pleased you enjoyed it. And it was a first for me too. I've never had sex in any kind of motor vehicle before now.'

It seemed every time Rhodri and I got together, we ticked off a new experience, a new fantasy. Maybe it was just as well this was destined to be nothing more than a brief affair. Or maybe we'd be one of those couples I'd always envied; those who managed to keep their relationship fresh and exciting, even after years together.

He ran a hand down my bare arm. 'Well, my mother always used to say you should always save the first time for the one you really love …'

The words caused me to stiffen, and without thinking, I pulled away from him. He looked at me but said nothing as I slipped the straps of my top back up my shoulders, and grabbed my skirt. The interior of the Land Rover smelled of sweat and sex, and the heat we'd generated between us still lingered. It was just as well Rhodri was taking the vehicle to be cleaned before his father took possession of it once more.

Don't start thinking about having some kind of future with this man, I chided myself. You know that's not going to happen, so why see this as anything but a beautiful memory you're creating: something to keep you warm on a cold winter's night. And most of all, don't give your heart to him, however much you might want to.

Nuzzling Rhodri's ear, I said, 'I don't know about you, but I've got a real appetite after that. How about fish and chips, my treat?'

'You're on,' he replied.

If he noticed my distant expression as we drove back towards Aberpentre, he didn't comment. Maybe he was too consumed with his own thoughts of what would happen when the time came for me to leave.

SEVENTEEN

Forcing myself to go into work after a date with Rhodri was always difficult, but today it had seemed impossible. Last night, when he'd taken me to that little, secluded bay and we'd walked hand in hand down to the sea it had seemed my love life was as close to perfect as it had ever come. I might well call the shots in the boardroom, but my relationships had never achieved anything like the same success. The boyfriends I'd had before Gavin had been largely forgettable, and after him, I'd become convinced that I would never find anyone suitable.

Rhodri was different; unlike all the other men I'd dated, he didn't move in the kind of circles or have the background and breeding that would have impressed my father. Yet despite that, I knew Dad would have liked him. His enthusiasm and drive was infectious, and he didn't look at me as if wondering what I could do for him: how he could use my money and connections to his advantage.

But then, I reflected, he didn't actually know me. He knew Jane. And that changed everything.

After we'd driven back from the bay, we'd stopped off to buy fish and chips. We'd sat on the sea wall and eaten them straight from the wrapping, chatting and laughing about everything and nothing. When I'd arrived in Aberpentre, I'd never believed that leaving the town behind would be a wrench, but now I knew that saying goodbye to Rhodri would be one of the most difficult things I'd ever had to do.

It was quiet on the front desk, so I took the opportunity to go through the feedback forms and note any comments regarding the provision of the "good night's sleep" kits to guests. Most of the people who'd used them appeared to have good things to say about the eye masks, but were less favourable when it came to the earplugs. Still, they seemed impressed by the general concept, with more than one person making a comment along the lines of "never been given anything like this in any other hotel", and adding that it would certainly encourage them to use the Anthony chain again.

At least that was one positive conversation I'd be having when I returned to head office. More difficult would be any discussion of the future of this particular hotel. I had serious work to do to convince the more sceptical members of the board that keeping a presence in Aberpentre would be cost effective. When looked at in the cold, unemotional terms of figures on a balance sheet, there was no argument. Renovating this place would be a long and expensive process, and there was no guarantee that occupancy rates would increase as a result. The building was of much more value as a piece of real estate, and logic dictated selling it.

Logic, though, didn't take into account all the people who would lose their jobs if the hotel were to close, or the impact of the town on yet another of its famous landmarks disappearing. Aberpentre might choose to look to the future, and the changes that urban regeneration could bring, but that didn't mean it had to dismiss its past out of hand.

Things would be clearer, I was sure, once I was back in London, and could arrange the meetings where all these matters could be thrashed out. For now, I just had to sit tight and try not to think about matters I couldn't currently influence.

Someone had left a copy of that morning's *Daily Express* open on one of the lobby tables, and I went to tidy it up. As I did, a headline on the business page caught my eye.

Golden State Scammer in Fraud Arrest.

Scooping up the newspaper, I took it back to the front desk. I pored through the story with a mounting sense of disbelief.

Property magnate Alastair Hammond, 46, was yesterday arrested in connection with a series of fraudulent business deals. Hammond, who also went by the aliases Al Harriott and Ally Haynes, was wanted by police in Britain, the United States, and Canada.

Hammond's company, Golden State Properties, ran an elaborate scam that targeted premises in areas undergoing urban regeneration, which they claimed they wanted to turn into upmarket apartment complexes. They offered a price significantly above current market values, but when contracts were exchanged, Hammond paid with forged cheques. Even while the original owners were attempting to reverse the transaction and regain control of their property, Golden State was already selling off-plan apartments in buildings they did not actually own...

So that was why the deal to buy the Anthony had seemed too generous to be true. Hammond hadn't been working some complicated tax evasion scheme, or looking to get his hands on money from the regeneration fund. He'd been a con man, pure and simple. He'd used people like my father to help him – albeit without their knowledge – fleece would-be homeowners of their money, taking deposits for apartments that would never be built. I could see how Dad, with his old-fashioned belief that everyone adhered to the same business ethics as he did, could so easily have been suckered by someone who told him exactly what he wanted to hear. Would I have seen through the man's lies, or would I have been too relieved that someone wanted to take the hotel off my hands to listen to my instincts?

'Jane, are you OK? You look like you've seen a ghost.'

Rhodri had appeared from nowhere. His hand was on my elbow, steadying me, as if he believed I might fall from my chair.

'No, I'm fine, honestly,' I replied, closing the paper before he could see what I'd been reading. Not that the names Alastair Hammond or Golden State would have meant anything to him, of course. 'I just felt a bit faint, that's all.'

'Maybe you should get some fresh air.' He dug in his pocket, pulled out his wallet and extracted a five-pound note. 'Tell you what, why don't you nip out and get us both a coffee. I could use a caffeine boost after the morning I'm having.'

'Bad news?'

His sigh told me more than words could. 'I've been on the phone to the insurance company for the last forty-five minutes. The motor in one of the washing machines in the laundry room has burned out. I reckon replacing it is covered under the terms of our policy, but they're trying to tell me it's classed as industrial wear and tear.'

'Well, when did you ever hear of any insurance company paying up unless they absolutely had to?'

'Tell me about it.' He turned on his heel and left the lobby, calling back over his shoulder, 'Add an apple turnover to my order. I'll be in my office when you get back.'

Thoughts of Hammond and his scam still occupied my mind as I walked to the sandwich shop. More specifically, I couldn't help thinking about his victims. Not just the people he'd conned out of their deposits, but all those who'd lost their jobs when the businesses in which they'd worked had been sold to Golden State. If Hammond's offer for the Anthony had been accepted, the same thing would have happened to Rhodri and all his staff – and all for nothing.

I didn't even want to consider how long it might have taken my father to reclaim the hotel once he discovered he'd been paid with a bad cheque, even with the top-quality team of lawyers he'd had at his disposal. As for the bad publicity that would have come in the wake of the deal collapsing, it would have made him a laughing stock in the business world. All things considered, the company had had a fortunate escape. I only wished Dad could still be around to appreciate it.

Maybe this was a sign that I shouldn't be thinking of selling the hotel. But just because Hammond's motives had been less than honourable, it didn't mean I couldn't find another developer who really was prepared to turn the

Anthony into homes – affordable ones, not the extravagant plans I'd seen for luxury apartments and gym facilities.

I really wanted to sit Kay down with a glass of wine and talk through the problem with her. She already knew that I had doubts over the future of the hotel, after all, and she had a way of cutting through all the nonsense surrounding any issue and getting straight to the core of it.

More than that, I wished I could tell her about Rhodri, and my fears that I was losing my heart to him. I couldn't fall in love with him, not now. At the right time, in the right place, he might very well be the best thing that ever happened to me. He turned me on like no man ever had, and I would have said he knew me better than any other man had too. Except he didn't really know me at all. He knew Jane, and that wasn't the same thing.

I looked up at the grey clouds that were scudding in over the bay, low and heavy with rain, and sent out a silent plea to the one other person in the world who could have given me the advice I needed.

Oh, Mum, what the hell have I got myself into?

EIGHTEEN

The bad weather had set in almost as soon as I returned to the Anthony with cappuccinos for Rhodri and myself, and I'd spent the rest of Friday afternoon and all of Saturday staring out of the lobby windows at the steadily falling rain.

A couple of times on Saturday evening, I'd reached for the digital recorder, about to put my thoughts down on tape, then stopped. The things I really wanted to discuss – the potential sale of the hotel to Golden State Properties, and how disastrous it would have been if the sale had been agreed, and my confused feelings over Rhodri – were both off-limits as far as my video confessions were concerned. I wasn't a Catholic, so I couldn't go down and unburden myself to my friendly neighbourhood priest, and while I was sure I could find a traditional gypsy fortune teller plying her trade somewhere on the prom, I doubted she'd really be able to tell me whether I had a future with the tall, dark stranger in my life.

Sunday dawned bright and fair, and I was just gathering up my dirty clothes and bed linen to take to the laundrette when the phone rang.

'Hey, Jane, how's it going?'

'Rhodri. It's lovely to hear from you, but shouldn't you be off returning your dad's Land Rover?'

'Already done it. He and Mum are taking the caravan up to Black Rock for a few days, so I had to make sure it was back nice and early so they could get off. Anyway, I just wondered if you fancied going out somewhere, maybe get something to eat.'

'What, right now?' I looked down at the sweatpants and baggy T-shirt I wore.

'Why not?'

'OK, but I'll need to have a quick shower and get changed.'

'No problem. I'll meet you outside the hotel in half an hour.'

By the time I joined Rhodri, my hair washed and hastily blow-dried, and wearing jeans and a white cardigan over my ditsy print top, the rainclouds were gathering once more.

'Do you think the weather's going to hold?' I asked, eyeing the filthy grey sky with suspicion.

'That's the joy of a Welsh summer,' Rhodri replied with a grin. 'You get to enjoy all four seasons in one day. So, where do you fancy going?'

'Surprise me.'

We'd almost reached the pier head when the rain began to fall. Cold, hard drops soaked through the wool of my cardigan. We dashed for the nearest available cover, huddling under the candy-striped awning over the entrance to Bellini's.

'Maybe we should go inside and grab a drink, wait for this to pass over,' Rhodri suggested.

Anxiety clutched at my belly. 'Won't Angharad be

working?'

'Not on a Sunday. She always goes to have lunch with her grandmother in Criccieth.'

'OK, it's just that I'm obviously not her favourite person around here, and I don't know how she'd react if I walked into her territory.'

'You'll be fine.' Rhodri hugged me to him. 'If she ever tries anything, she'll have me to deal with.'

Soft piano music greeted us as we looked around for seats. The small bar was surprisingly full for a Sunday lunchtime, and I realised we weren't the only ones who'd decided to seek shelter here from the rain. Rhodri spotted two vacant stools by the bar, and we made our way over to claim them.

The bartender was busy mixing something in a silver cocktail shaker, tossing it up in the air and catching it one-handed, with a nonchalance Tom Cruise would have been proud of.

'He fancies himself a bit, doesn't he?' I commented.

Rhodri reached for the drinks menu. 'Yeah, but I bet it earns him some fantastic tips.'

'I've got a tip for him.' I grinned, as the bartender sent the cocktail shaker spinning through the air once more. 'Whatever you do, don't drop that thing.'

'What are you in the mood for?' Rhodri pushed the menu across the bar counter so I could study it.

I could give him an answer to that, but it didn't involve alcohol. 'You know, I'd love a Bloody Mary.'

'Good idea. I think I'll have the same.'

He looked up, hoping to attract the bartender's attention, just as a familiar figure arrived to set down a tray of used glasses on the counter.

'Still waiting for that Long Island Iced Tea for the table in the corner,' Angharad snapped at the bartender.

'Coming right up,' the man replied. He unscrewed the top of the shaker and prepared to pour the contents into a large glass jug.

For the first time, Angharad appeared to notice us. 'Well, fancy seeing you here, Rhodri … Jane.' Her tone was noticeably colder as she addressed me.

'I didn't expect you to be working today.' Rhodri was trying his best to keep the atmosphere pleasant between us all. 'You not having lunch with your nan?'

'She's in Bryn Maris hospital, for a hip replacement.' The look Angharad shot me as she spoke left me with the strangest feeling that this was somehow my fault. 'I'm off up there to see here when I finish my shift.'

'Well, send her my best wishes,' Rhodri said.

'I will. That's why Nan always liked you. So thoughtful …' Seeming to remember her job involved more than just making small talk with her ex-boyfriend, Angharad pulled a small pad and a pen from her apron pocket. 'So, what are you having, Rhodri?'

'Two Bloody Marys, please.'

'Coming right up.' She scribbled the order on her pad and went to place it with the bartender. I half expected her to ask him to slip a dose of rat poison into mine.

'Well, that was awkward,' I said, watching Angharad delivering the pitcher of Long Island Iced Tea to the party in the corner.

'She's harmless, really,' Rhodri assured me. 'And once we've had this drink, we'll go somewhere else.'

For all I'd mocked the bartender's flashy style, the man knew how to mix a drink. The Bloody Mary had just the right balance of vodka to tomato juice, enhanced by a spicy kick from the Tabasco and Worcestershire sauces. As I sipped the delicious cocktail, it was easy to ignore the odd malicious glance Angharad shot my way. What did it matter? She couldn't do anything to hurt me, not really.

When she brought the bill, I waved away Rhodri's attempts to pay. If nothing else, that might help to convince her I wasn't some kind of gold digger, only spending time with my boss because of what he might be able to do for my career prospects.

Rhodri's joking references to Wales's changeable weather hadn't been too wide of the mark. As we walked away from the wine bar, the sun came out from behind a cloud, its light so bright it dazzled my eyes.

I shoved a hand into my bag to fish out my sunglasses. They weren't there. Neither, I realised with a sick flip of my stomach, was my purse.

'Rhodri, I can't find my purse. I think I must have left it in Bellini's.'

'OK, let's go back and look for it. Hopefully one of the staff might have seen you walk off without it.'

I dashed back in the direction we'd come, hideous possibilities whirling in my mind. The worst of them wasn't that the purse had gone for good, and I'd have to get on the phone to my bank and cancel all my cards, but that someone might look inside and wonder why the name on those cards didn't match that of the woman who carried them around.

I'd only gone a few yards when I almost collided with Angharad. Her smile was cold and unfriendly, but I didn't read anything out of the ordinary into that.

'I think you forgot something.' She held my purse in

her hand.

'Oh, thanks so much, Angharad. I was hoping someone would find that for me.'

'No, I don't mean the purse.' She timed her next words so they would be the first thing Rhodri heard as he joined us. 'I mean, you forgot to mention that you don't actually appear to be called Jane.'

'What are you talking about?' Rhodri appeared baffled. He must have assumed that his ex was simply attempting to create more drama.

Angharad opened the purse, and pulled out a couple of cards. 'Well, this –' she held up my credit card '– is in the name of Claudia Anthony. And so is this, and this …' She paused, clearly revelling in my discomfort. 'And I started to think that maybe someone other than Jane had left this purse behind, even though I'd seen you take it out of your bag to pay the bill. So I wondered what kind of stunt you were pulling, and then I found this …'

She drew a final item from the purse. I knew what it would be even before she brandished it, but she strung the moment out, enjoying her triumph.

Angharad handed over my company security pass to Rhodri. Even though I had blonde hair in the photo, he'd seen me without glasses enough times that the resemblance could not be denied. My cover had been well and truly blown.

'You – you're Claudia Anthony?' Rhodri gaped at me. He gave my pass one last, disbelieving look before handing it over to me. 'Do you want to tell me just what the hell is going on?'

I glanced from him to Angharad, who stood with her arms folded and a self-satisfied smirk on her lips. There was no point trying to brazen it out; I had to tell the truth.

'Yes, I'm Claudia. I came to Aberpentre to film a documentary, like I said, but it's nothing to do with women struggling to find work or retraining for a new career. I'm working undercover in the hotel for an edition of *Secret CEO*, and that's why I had to use a false identity.'

'So what you're saying is that you came here to spy on me … on everyone at the hotel?' When Rhodri put it like that, it sounded terrible, but that wasn't what I'd been doing.

'No, not spying. If I'd come here as the boss of Anthony Hotels, you'd all have been on your best behaviour, anxious to make a good impression on me. You wouldn't have been honest about the problems you've been having, and I certainly wouldn't have been able to make an accurate assessment of what needs to be done to improve the hotel's fortunes. As it is, I was planning to go back to London and make sure you get better computers so the booking system doesn't crash all the time, and find the money in the budget to replace the lift before anyone else gets stuck in it … Come on, Rhodri, you can't tell me those things wouldn't make your life easier.'

'Of course they would, but I don't want to get them just because Miss Hotshot CEO comes down to Wales and feels sorry for us. It must have been awful to discover how backward and primitive we all are here.'

'Oh come on, now you're just being ridiculous. Do you want the other option, which is that I go back to London and tell the board we might just as well cut our losses with the hotel and sell it to a property developer, because the way things stand, I'm just as inclined to do that.'

I gave Rhodri a moment to let that piece of information sink in. 'Do what you want, Jane – Claudia – whatever the hell your name really is. I don't care. I only wish you'd had the guts to tell me the truth before now. It might have spared both of us a lot of heartache.'

'If I'd told you the truth, would you have believed me?'

His face contorted with an expression I didn't like. 'Look, all I know is that I don't want you setting foot in the hotel again, even if you do own the damn thing. And if that documentary appears on TV, I will sue you and the production company for every penny you've got. Forget whatever release documents they've got; I signed those under false pretences, and you know it.'

He couldn't mean any of that; it was pride and anger talking, not the Rhodri I'd come to know so well. 'Come on, Rhodri, calm down. We can talk about this.'

'Oh no, I think we've done all the talking we're going to do.'

With that, he turned and walked away. I didn't make any attempt to go after him, certain he wouldn't listen to me whatever I tried to tell him. Already, tears pricked at my eyes, and I didn't want to give Angharad the pleasure of seeing me cry.

I snatched my belongings from Angharad's grip. 'I hope you're happy now.'

'Oh, I'm absolutely delirious. But then I always like to see someone get what they deserve.'

I knew I shouldn't sink to her level, but I couldn't help it. 'Well, before you start gloating, how likely is it that Rhodri's going to hang around in this poxy little town when we close the Anthony? If you seriously believe he's got any intention of going back to you now, you must be living on another planet. You think you've sabotaged me – are you sure you haven't just sabotaged yourself in the process?'

Without really being aware of which direction I walked in, I found myself back at Bay Vista. I couldn't believe I'd been so stupid. I'd given Angharad all the ammunition she needed to destroy my relationship with Rhodri, as well as the documentary. There was no way we could complete the filming of *Secret CEO*, not with my cover story in tatters. I'd wasted nearly three weeks of my life; time I could have spent arranging the sale of the Aberpentre hotel and its assets. Why were we hanging on to this relic from another age? Dad had been right; we should have made the right decision and disposed of the property long ago. It had broken my heart twice over; once when I'd seen the state it had been allowed to fall into, and the strain that placed on the people who worked there, and again when I'd let myself get so close to the man who managed it. That had been the biggest mistake of all.

A voice in the back of my head nagged at me. I had to let someone at Wild Card know what had happened, but I really didn't want to speak to Hugo Murray. I could only guess at what his reaction would be.

'Jane, I haven't seen you for a while.' Gaynor Rhys's friendly tones distracted me from my despair. 'Everything OK?'

'Fine, thank you.' I spoke with a cheerfulness I didn't feel. 'I've just been working really hard. The documentary, you know ...'

'Well, I shall be sorry to see you go. And the lads in Room 4 too. That Bayo's such a nice young man. I'll miss him.'

I'm sure you will. I found myself stifling a grin, recalling Dean's stories of Gaynor and her relentless pursuit of his friend with baked goods. But her words had also decided my course of action.

'I'm sure he'll miss you too,' I assured her. Before she could settle in for a chat, I added, 'I'll see you later, Gaynor,' and headed for the stairs that led to Apartment 4.

I took a deep breath, steadying myself, before knocking. 'Hang on!' came the call from inside. A moment later, Dean answered the door. He had wet hair, and wore only a towel around his waist. From the bathroom came the sound of running water.

'Oh, I'm sorry. I didn't mean to get you out of the shower. I'll come back later.'

Something in my tone must have alerted him to the fact something was wrong. 'No, that's OK, babe. Come in. Take a seat.'

I made myself comfortable on the low, black leather sofa. Dean padded off to the shower, where he turned off the water. He appeared to be alone in the apartment.

'Bayo not with you?' I asked as he came to join me.

'He's just nipped out for a packet of cigarettes. Is everything OK?'

I shook my head. 'No, something really awful's happened. Rhodri's found out who I really am, and I've ruined your show …' My voice cracked; I couldn't go on. The tears that had been threatening since I'd argued with Rhodri started to flow, and I brushed them from my cheeks.

'Hey, Claudia, it's OK. Don't cry.' Dean sat beside me and wrapped an arm round my shoulder. Though his skin

226

was still damp from the shower, his hug was comforting, and I didn't pull away. 'I'll make you a cup of tea and you can let me know exactly what happened.'

He spent the next couple of minutes bustling around in the kitchen. I sat and listened to the sound of the kettle boiling, and cupboard doors being opened. Whatever happened, I still had friends here, I reminded myself.

'Here you go.' Dean returned with a mug in each hand, and set one on the coffee table before me. When I took a sip, it was stronger than I'd expected, and he'd added sugar. Right now, it was just what I needed.

'Thanks,' I murmured.

'Hot, sweet tea. It really is the remedy for everything.' He sat once more, and drank from his own mug. 'Now, tell me everything.'

'OK …' I let out a soft sigh, wondering where to begin. 'Rhodri and I went for a drink at Bellini's, down by the pier head. And when we left, I realised I didn't have my purse.'

'What, you mean it was stolen? Have you let the police know?'

'No, I got it back. I'd left it on the bar and someone saw me walk out without it. The only trouble is that someone was Rhodri's bitch of an ex-girlfriend.' I cradled the tea mug in my hands, recalling the gleam of triumph in Angharad's eyes when she'd brandished the purse. 'Anyone else might have just had a quiet word with me, asked why my ID is in the name of Claudia Anthony when they know me as Jane. But not Angharad. She just wanted to humiliate me in front of Rhodri. Well, she did that, all right.'

'So she revealed your real identity to him?'

I nodded, feeling a hard lump rise in my throat. Swallowing it down, I went on, 'He didn't take it very well, to put it mildly. Accused me of deliberately lying to him. And now he doesn't want anything to do with me – or the documentary. In fact, he's threatening to sue us for misrepresentation, or some nonsense like that.'

'Forgive me if I'm reading too much into this, but this "drink" –' setting down his mug, Dean made air quotes around the word '– you and Rhodri were having. Would this have been more of a date?'

I couldn't lie to Dean. 'Yes. We've been seeing each other for the last couple of weeks.'

He raised an eyebrow. 'Well, you've kept that quiet, haven't you?'

'I had to. Don't think I didn't want to tell you, but much as I love you, Dean, you have a big mouth.'

He put a hand to his chest in a theatrical gesture, as if wounded by the accusation, but we both knew it to be true. If I'd shared my secret with him, he'd have blabbed it at some point, most likely without meaning to.

'Can you imagine how Hugo would have reacted if he'd found out? He'd have had you and Bayo tailing me, trying to get compromising footage of Rhodri and me together. Everything you'd shot so far would be edited to make it look like the romance of the century. Either that or he'd have found some way to manufacture another confrontation between us, like he did with that chambermaid business. The programme wouldn't be about the hotel any more; it would be about my love life, and I didn't want that.'

'Well, I can't say I blame you.'

'I'm really sorry that this has happened now, when so

much of the filming's been completed. I just feel like I've wasted everybody's time.'

'Not everybody's.' Dean gave an apologetic grin. 'I had a lovely couple of days with Maurice in Chester, and I wouldn't be starting to plan my wedding arrangements if I hadn't been working on this project.'

The door opened, and Bayo strode into the room. He looked from a half-dressed Dean to me, and back. 'What have I missed?'

'Rhodri knows I'm actually Claudia Anthony. Some kind soul decided to reveal my identity to him. I was just telling Dean there's no way we can finish the filming, not now.'

Dean's expression clearly said, "That's not all you were telling me," but he kept quiet. If Bayo were to discover I'd been dating Rhodri, then that information would come from my lips.

'So where is Rhodri now?' Bayo asked.

'I don't know. At home, most likely.'

'We need to get hold of him. There's bound to be a way we can salvage this.'

'You really think so?' My tone was sceptical.

'Yeah, this isn't the first time someone's disguise has been seen through. Dean, remember the guy who ran that haulage firm – what was his name?'

'Oh yes, that could have got very messy.'

'We sorted that out, and we'll sort this too,' Bayo said confidently. 'Don't worry, Claudia. I'm sure we can make Rhodri see sense about this.'

Dean's phone lay on the table. He picked it up, and scrolled down till he found the number he wanted.

I found myself holding my breath as I waited for the

call to be answered. 'Hey, Rhodri. It's Dean Parker here. Can you talk right now …? Yeah, that's great. Look, I need to have a word with you. No, no, it's nothing serious. Is it OK if I come over to see you …?'

He was going to say no. I just knew it. Rhodri had to know I'd spoken to Dean. If he didn't want to speak to me, he certainly wouldn't want to speak to my cameraman.

To my surprise, I heard Dean saying, 'Let me just make a note of your address …' He gestured to Bayo, who went to grab a ballpoint pen from the mantelpiece and tossed it to Dean. Dean scribbled the address on the top sheet of a block of Post-It Notes that lay on the table. 'OK, be there in about fifteen minutes. Yeah, see you then.'

'I can't believe you got him to agree to that,' I said, impressed by Dean's decisive manner.

'See, I can be a diplomat when I need to. Now, just give me a couple of minutes to get dressed, then we're going over to Rhodri's.'

'We?' I repeated.

'Of course. Do you want to clear the air with him or not?'

'Yes, but isn't he going to be angry when he realises you've tricked him?'

Dean was already on his way to the bedroom. He turned his head and shot the words, 'Nothing we can't handle,' over his shoulder.

I could only hope his confidence wasn't misplaced.

NINETEEN

The look Rhodri gave me as he opened the door to us made it clear I was the last person he wanted to see.

'May we come in?' Dean asked.

'You and Bayo, yes. But not her. She stays outside in the car.'

'Either you speak to us all, or you don't speak to any of us,' Dean told him firmly. 'Look, Rhodri, Claudia's told us everything, and we really need to sort this out.'

'There's nothing to sort.' Rhodri spoke with the tone of a man who believed he'd said all he had to on the subject. 'I've been made a fool of, and I don't appreciate it.'

'OK, so people might not have been entirely honest with you, but –' A curtain twitched in the front window of the house next door, and Dean pushed at Rhodri's door, attempting to force his way inside. 'We can have this conversation on the doorstep if you'd like, but I'm sure you'd rather not have all the neighbours watching us.'

Rhodri's shoulders sagged, and he stood back to let us inside.

The kitchen door stood ajar, and I caught a glimpse of the table on which Rhodri had pleasured me. I'd never thought that when I came back to the house it would be under such sorry circumstances.

We went into the lounge. I sat on the sofa, Dean taking the seat next to me. Bayo leant against the doorframe, arms folded.

Rhodri paced the floor. 'Go on, all of you, say your piece. It's not going to make me change my mind.'

'Rhodri, mate, I know you're upset about everything that's happened –'

'Upset?' Rhodri cut in. 'I'm bloody furious. I gave you free rein to film in the hotel because I thought you were making a documentary about women who can't find jobs. And all the time, you were lying to me and she –' he jabbed a finger in my direction '– was planning to sell the place, knowing I didn't have a clue what her real motives were.'

'But you understand why we couldn't tell you what we were doing, don't you?' Dean said. 'Why you couldn't know that Claudia's really your boss?'

'The show's called *Secret CEO*. The clue's in the name,' Bayo added. Even though my world still felt like it was ending, my lips curved in a smile.

'You seem to think we were trying to trick you,' Dean went on, 'but this was never about making you, or anyone at the Anthony, look bad. This isn't about stitching you up when the programme is edited. How it works is that the person whose mistakes get shown is the boss; that's what the viewers want to see, because it makes them feel better about themselves if they think the people at the top are incompetent.' He spread his hands in supplication. 'You're a decent guy, Rhodri, so drop all this nonsense about suing and let us get on with doing our job.'

'Please, Rhodri.' For the first time, I spoke up. 'Can't

you see that Angharad did what she did out of pure spite? She just wanted to ruin things between you and me, and she seems to have managed that.'

'I'm sorry,' Rhodri said, 'this has just been a lot to take in. I'm going to need time to think about it.'

He sounded less certain than he had, and I sensed he was taking a mental step back from his initial rash proclamations. Maybe Dean was right and we could salvage the documentary.

'Well, perhaps it's best if we leave you to it. Let you sleep on it, and you can give us your decision in the morning.' Dean rose from the sofa.

I made to follow him. Rhodri took a quick step forward to catch hold of my hand. 'Don't go. We still have things to talk about.'

Bayo shot me a look. He seemed to have taken on the role of my protector, but by now I was beginning to think I had a reply to whatever accusations Rhodri might throw at me. Grateful as I was to both Bayo and Dean for their help and support, I felt I could manage without them. I nodded, letting him know that it would be OK to leave me here.

'You know where we are if you need us, Claudia,' Dean said.

'Thanks,' I replied softly.

The sound of the front door slamming let Rhodri and I know we were alone.

'So what did you need to say to me you couldn't say in front of the boys?' I asked.

Rhodri put his hands to his temples and pressed his elbows together, his face a mask of bewilderment. 'I just don't know what to think any more. When I found out who you were, I was so angry. I couldn't believe you would deceive me like that – you, of all people.'

'That's what this is really all about, isn't it? The fact that you and I had grown so close. Did you think I was just doing that for the sake of the show, so you'd be nicer to me? Because if you did, then you're right. You don't really know who I am.'

'It's not like that. What I said the other night, about falling in love with you … I meant it. But I thought I was talking to Jane, and now I know she doesn't actually exist, I feel like I've been taken for a fool.'

'Rhodri, please don't talk like that. I never meant to hurt you. How do you think I felt, knowing that at the end of the filming, I'd have to reveal my real identity to you? I've been falling for you too, but it's been so hard, trying to deny the way I felt and knowing that I couldn't make any promises to you because we'd have no future together.' I picked up my handbag, and slung the strap over my shoulder. 'So go on, do whatever you have to do. I'm sure we'll all survive, whatever happens. And if I put the Anthony on the market, remember that I'm making a business decision, not a personal one.'

I turned to leave, but Rhodri pulled me to him. 'Claudia, don't go. I don't want it to end like this.' His voice cracked. 'If I'm honest, I don't want it to end at all.'

'But …'

'But nothing.' The touch of his lips on mine stopped any further talk, and ignited feelings I'd fought so hard to damp down. Call me weak, call me foolish, but all my resolve melted in the face of that kiss.

'Should we be doing this?' I asked, when we eventually broke apart.

'I don't care if you don't,' he replied. 'I thought I could

234

let you go, but I can't, no matter who you are.'

He grabbed my hand and started to lead me to his bedroom, but we only made it as far as the hall before we were kissing again. Rhodri unbuttoned my cardigan and pushed it off my shoulders, so he could nibble at the bare expanse of my shoulders and collarbone. I pushed my hands up under his top, stroking over the warm planes of his lower back.

We made a slow ascent of the stairs, shedding clothes as we went. By the time we reached the landing, I had on only my little lacy boy shorts, and Rhodri a pair of black briefs with the designer's name embroidered in white on the waistband. Rhodri hoisted me up and carried me into the bedroom, my arms locked around the back of his neck and his hands gripping my bum. Our progress was less than steady, as we kept on pecking at each other's lips, and he stumbled, dropping rather than lowering me on to the bed.

I lay sprawled on the mattress, looking up at him, wondering how all the anger and tension had dissipated into this awkward but anxious need for each other. What was it they said about the best part of breaking up being making up? Except Rhodri had broken up with Jane and was making up with Claudia. This was all far too confusing.

He took off my glasses, and held them to his eyes for a moment before setting them down. I knew he'd worked out they were purely cosmetic. 'So, the morning you almost left these behind ...'

'Let's not talk about that right now. Not when we have more pressing matters to attend to.' I reached out to trail a finger over the prominent bulge in his briefs. 'Lie back,

Rhodri, and let me say sorry to you in the nicest way I know.'

I kissed my way along his body, rubbing myself against him as I went. In turn, I sucked each of his nipples between my lips, nipping at the little buds until they formed hard peaks, and down his flat stomach.

His excitement was all too obvious as I reached for the waistband of his briefs. As I peeled the fabric down and off, his cock uncoiled, rising up to greet me. Such a beautiful sight, and all mine.

At first, I ignored that straining length, concentrating instead and the sensitive place just above the mat of hair around the base of his shaft. I circled my tongue over his skin, taking my time, enjoying the taste and feel of him. He hadn't showered since he'd left me outside Bellini's, and I relished the salt of his sweat and his earthy, masculine scent. When I looked up at Rhodri's face, he was biting his full lower lip and his eyes were half-closed in bliss. He seemed to approve of the way I'd chosen to apologise.

I moved lower, sensing rather than hearing his soft sighs as I brushed my tongue over the seam between them. He writhed against the sheets, muttering something that sounded like, 'Can't ... need ...'

Taking the tip of his cock between my lips, I flicked it with the point of my tongue. Rhodri groaned, and tried to push more of himself into my mouth, but my hand was wrapped firmly around his length, giving me control of how deeply I took him. I lapped at his crown, licking up the salty droplets that leaked from his crown.

My own need was growing, my juices soaking through my lacy shorts, and I knew that if I kept on worshipping

Rhodri with my mouth he would come before either of us was ready. If I remembered rightly, he kept condoms in his bedside drawer, and I let him slip from my grasp as I rose to retrieve one.

Once I had him safely sheathed, I went to climb on top of him, but Rhodri had other ideas. He rolled me onto my back and spread my legs wide, then settled in between them. I gazed up, my eyes never leaving his as he thrust home, filling me with one easy stroke. It felt like he was coming home, and tears almost came to my eyes once more as I thought how close we'd been to throwing this all away.

Then there was nothing but the feel of his skin against mine, two bodies moving as one. The sighs and the heat and the urgency of our passion filled the little bedroom; we seemed lost in our own private world. I was rocked by a sudden, shattering orgasm. I clung to Rhodri like I was seeking salvation from the storm, but even through the roaring of the blood in my ears, I heard the word he called at the point of his own climax.

'Claudia.'

EPILOGUE

'Morning, *cariad* ...'

I came awake to the sound of Rhodri's voice, his breath warm against my ear. Rolling over, I looked at the clock on the bedside table and realised it was close to 11 o'clock. I didn't usually sleep so late on a Sunday morning, but then I didn't usually spend my Saturday night making love to the most gorgeous man in the world.

'I thought about waking you, but you looked so peaceful,' he said. 'So I made you coffee and heated up some croissants.'

He set a tray down on the nightstand, moving the stuffed toy he'd won for me on Aberpentre pier out of the way. I'd never been so sentimental as to surround myself with the love tokens my other boyfriends had given me, but somehow that rabbit had come to stand for all that was good between Rhodri and me.

I breathed in the delicious aromas of freshly brewed hazelnut coffee and hot, buttery pastry and gave a contented sigh.

'You know just how to spoil me,' I told him, reaching up to drop a kiss on his stubbled cheek. 'And that's why I love you, Rhodri Wynn-Jones.'

It was difficult to believe how much things had changed since Angharad sparked that terrible confrontation outside Bellini's. Rhodri and I had woken the next morning, twined in each other's arms. I'd worried that once the passion of the night before had burned itself out, he might still harbour some resentment over the way I'd deceived him. But he seemed to realise that all his talk of legal action had been over the top, and he told me he drop his objections to the show being broadcast.

Not that Rhodri's change of heart meant there were no longer any problems to sort out. Once Hugo Murray learnt that my real identity had been discovered, he'd gone into damage limitation mode. Never mind that there'd still been over a week of the filming schedule left to complete, he ordered Dean, Bayo, and me back to London immediately. That didn't concern me too much – the novelty of being followed by a camera crew had worn off within days of me arriving in Aberpentre, and I'd started to look forward to the day I could pick up my normal life again. But I hated the feeling that Rhodri had been left in the lurch, and it had been my fault. It would be easy enough to find someone from the temp agency to cover the front desk job. What really concerned me was the unfinished business he and I had between us.

Four days after I'd returned to work in head office, Rhodri, Tom, and Wioletta had been brought down to London so we could film the scenes in which I revealed to them that I was Claudia Anthony, not Jane Ennis. Though Rhodri already knew the truth, he'd sworn not to let the others in on the secret, and judging by their reactions when they walked into my office, he'd kept his word. And even he'd worn a genuine expression of shock on seeing

Jane's brown hair transformed back into Claudia's long, honey-gold locks. That, however, was just a temporary transformation, as I'd already reached the conclusion that while blondes might have more fun, I preferred myself as a brunette.

One by one, I'd spoken to each member of Rhodri's staff, explaining to them what I'd learnt during my spell at the Anthony, and how their help and guidance had shaped my experience of working undercover. Wioletta just greeted my revelations with a wry shake of her head, as if she should have realised all along that I wasn't who I claimed to be. When I told her that, despite my claims to have no experience of cleaning rooms, I'd actually spent a summer working as a chambermaid, she just murmured, 'I knew it. I thought all along you were too good for a novice.' But she didn't seem resentful that she'd been tricked, and her face broke into the most whole-hearted smile I'd seen from her when I said we wanted her to help us shape the standards and practices for the housekeeping teams across all our hotels, with the resulting increase in salary that her consultant role would bring.

'Wioletta, Anthony Hotels always aims to reward the best,' I'd told her. 'And trust me, you're the best.'

Next up was Tom, who looked around as if this was all some kind of prank directed at him, and at any moment his friends would jump out and announce they couldn't believe he'd fallen for it. Once I'd convinced him that I genuinely did run the business, and he wasn't going to end up on some late-night compilation of viral internet clips, I went on to explain what we were prepared to do for him.

'Tom, I look at you and I see someone who has a lot of potential to progress within the company. I was impressed by the calm way you dealt with the fire alarm and the evacuation process, and I appreciated your efforts to make me feel a welcome part of the staff. Rhodri's told me that you're off to study business management in Cardiff, and what I'd like to do when you complete your course is put you on our fast-track scheme for graduate recruits. Who knows, you could be running one of our flagship hotels by the time you're Rhodri's age.'

When Tom had left the office, still looking slightly dazed, Rhodri had taken his place in the hot seat. The moment he'd walked in, I'd sensed the same electric tension in the air I always felt when he was around. There was so much I wanted to talk to him about, so much that had been left unsaid between us, but Hugo, still concerned about the integrity of his documentary, had told me not to contact any of the hotel staff before they arrived at my office.

It had been so difficult to treat him as just another employee, when what I wanted more than anything was to fall into his arms and apologise again for having to lie to him. But I'd kept our conversation polite and professional.

'Rhodri, I have to admit that when I arrived at the Anthony in Aberpentre, given everything I knew about the state of the hotel and its occupancy rates, I knew I'd have some serious thinking to do about its future. And my initial impressions weren't favourable. But even though its refurbishment had fallen a long way down our list of priorities, that doesn't excuse the fact you have to run your booking system on computers that weren't designed to handle it – or that you have a lift which is so unreliable you have to warn guests against using it. I apologise on behalf of the company for those things, and everything else that makes your job so much harder than it needs to be.'

'I appreciate that,' Rhodri had replied, but he'd kept looking at me expectantly, wondering what else might be to come. The various members of the Anthony's staff had been deliberately kept separated throughout this interview process, so none of them would know what I'd said to the others. Though nothing that I'd said to Wioletta or Tom had given them any clue that I might have been considering the sale of the hotel.

'Now,' I'd gone on, 'those are small considerations, compared to the biggest question of all. I've had to weigh up whether or not the hotel has a future within the company, given the expense involved in bringing it up to the standard of the rest of the chain.' I did my best to keep my expression neutral. 'I've done a lot of thinking, and I've spoken to my board of directors, and we've come to the conclusion that the Anthony will get the facelift it needs.'

Rhodri had given a small, surprised gasp, and I knew it wasn't the news he'd been expecting to hear. 'That's fantastic. Thank you so much. But – but what changed your mind? Because everything you've said up to now tells me you were going to close the place down.'

'The staff had a lot to do with it. Even though the conditions weren't ideal, they just put up with them, and did what they could to make sure that guests had an enjoyable stay. And an attitude like that comes from the top. From what I've seen, you work hard to set a good example, Rhodri, and people follow your lead.'

A blush rose to his cheeks. 'I've always tried my best,' he muttered, responding to the unexpected compliment.

'But it's not just that. The longer I spent in Aberpentre, the more I realised how important it was that the town hangs on to what made it special, or no one will see any reason to stay there. One of the things I discovered in the course of my research was that the whole Llŷn Peninsula is receiving a sizeable payment from the European regeneration fund. I thought at first that money would only be available if you were starting up a new business, but it turns out that, given the Anthony's historical importance to the town, we can apply to the body that awards grants for heritage projects, and that will help cover our costs for the restoration of the exterior of the hotel.' I'd smiled, watching the play of emotions cross his face as the news sank in. 'It might also interest you to know that another of those heritage grants is going to be used to restore the drinking fountain on the sea front, though I don't think it'll be able to do anything to make the water taste better.'

'So when is all this going to start?' Rhodri had asked. 'And how long is it likely to take?'

'For a project of this size? We're looking at a good twelve months, if not longer. It'll have to be completed in stages, obviously, because we don't want to shut the hotel down entirely for that length of time, and the bulk of the work will be done in the winter. But the first things we'll be doing are getting new computers installed, and replacing the lift.'

Rhodri had shaken his head in disbelief and delight. He'd walked into my office expecting to hear that he was out of a job, so I could only imagine how he might be reacting to this news.

When the cameras had stopped rolling, I'd left my office to speak to Tom, Wioletta, and Rhodri before they

244

returned to Wales. Unsure of how they would all treat me now my secret was out, I was relieved to discover that Wioletta and Tom were genuinely grateful for the opportunities I'd offered them. Finding myself being enveloped in a huge hug by the Polish woman, who usually kept her emotions tightly in check, was a little alarming, but it seemed as if she bore no grudge over how I'd deceived her.

'And what about us, Rhodri?' I'd asked, as we stood looking into each other's eyes. I'd led him into the unoccupied boardroom, so we could talk without being disturbed. 'Are we still friends?'

'I think so.' He'd taken my hand, and traced soft circles over my palm with the pad of his thumb. 'We could even try being more than that, if you'd like. I said I was falling in love with you, but that was when I thought you were Jane. I'd like to see if I could fall in love with Claudia too.'

'I'd like that,' I'd assured him. 'I'm really not so very different to her, I promise, even if I am in charge of all this –' I swept out my free arm, in a gesture that encompassed not only the boardroom but also what it stood for.

'That doesn't worry me so much. It's more that I'm not sure how long it'll take to get used to you as a blonde.'

'Don't worry, that may not be permanent.' I'd grinned at his confused look. 'And I know it's going to be difficult, with you in Wales and me here in London, but if we really want to make this work, we will. We'll probably have to take it slowly at first, but perhaps that's for the best.'

His only answer had been put his lips to mine and give me a soft, sweet kiss. And that's when I'd started to believe that things really could work out between us, after all.

That had been six weeks ago. For all we'd talked about going slowly, taking time to get to know one another all over again, Rhodri and I had been messaging each other even before he'd arrived back in Aberpentre. We'd talked almost every night on the phone, our conversations starting in a chatty, friendly fashion, but gradually becoming every bit as explicit as the one I'd shared with him the day after we'd been stuck in the lift. We discussed all the things we would do to each other the next time we met; shared all our naughtiest thoughts and fantasies. The fears I'd entertained that, having known me as unemployed novice Jane, Rhodri would struggle to relate to high-flying Claudia appeared to be unfounded.

Just as I'd predicted, finding time to be together was proving more difficult. My work schedule was booked solid, and even if I managed to clear all my meetings for a couple of days, I still had to factor in the length of the journey to Aberpentre.

Rhodri had come up with the perfect solution, hiring a car so he could drive down to see me. He told me he'd thought of borrowing his Dad's Land Rover again, but wasn't sure about the practicalities of parking such a cumbersome vehicle on the crowded streets of London. Returning to Aberpentre with scrapes in the paintwork or a missing rear light was the perfect way to ensure he was never allowed behind the wheel again.

'You'll be fine,' I told him airily. 'I have my own allocated parking space if I need to use it.' And then I'd thought of Rhodri's cosy little terraced house, and wondered what he'd think of the contrast to my apartment block, with its uniformed concierge and its underground garage.

I'd planned for us to take a river trip along the Thames so he could get the best view of the sights before going out to dinner, but Rhodri seemed more than happy to spend the weekend in the apartment, living off takeaway food from the nearby Italian deli and getting to know my body all over again. And last night, we'd had sex in every position we could think of, and fallen asleep in each other's arms as dawn was breaking.

The message light on my phone was blinking. I reached for it through sheer force of habit, and checked to see who'd been in touch while Rhodri poured coffee for us both.

'Hugo at Wild Card has just sent me an email,' I informed him. 'They're airing my episode of *Secret CEO* next Monday night at eight.'

'And will you watching it?'

'Absolutely not. I don't even intend to be in the country, if I can help it.' I sat up in bed as an idea occurred to me. 'Rhodri, when was the last time you took a proper break from work?'

He shrugged. 'I dunno. Not for a couple of years, I don't think. Couple of mates and I went to Glastonbury, but it pissed it down all weekend, so I wouldn't exactly class that as a holiday.'

'Well, don't you think you're overdue one, then?' I reached for my phone, and opened up a flight-booking app.

'What are you doing?' Rhodri asked, peering over my

shoulder as I scrolled down the list of destinations.

'I've made an executive decision. You're taking a fortnight off to recharge your batteries, and we're going on a holiday abroad, preferably somewhere they don't have TV or Wi-Fi and if you say the words *Secret CEO* they just look at you with blank incomprehension.'

'I can't,' he said, even though his expression showed he was tempted by the prospect. 'Who's going to run the hotel in my absence?'

'You'll find someone. Maybe this could be Tom's opportunity to get some hands-on experience, find out what it's really like to be in charge before he goes off to start his course.'

'I suppose so ...' His tone softened. 'Say we did go away somewhere. Where exactly did you have in mind?'

'Well, The Maldives would be nice at this time of year.' I closed my eyes, picturing soft white sand, endless blue sea, and the two of us curled together in a hammock, sipping cocktails from coconut shells as we watched the sun go down. 'Though I suppose it doesn't really matter where we go,' I added, as Rhodri slipped his hand over my hip and started to caress the slight curve of my belly, 'because if this turns into the kind of holiday I hope it will, I don't think we'll ever get as far as leaving the bedroom ...'

The Darkness Within Him

The Untwisted Series #1

A dizzying, all consuming affair with famous pianist Nicholas Jackson drew in bookshop owner Rebecca Langley, engulfed her with his passion and dominance, and then spat her out heartbroken and bruised.

Now, Rebecca is left trying to move on from the relationship she shared with Nicholas, but just as she starts to clear her head, he reappears in her life determined to win her back.

But seeing as Nicholas has already shown once that the darkness within him is lurking just below the surface, can Rebecca really take that risk again with her heart and body?